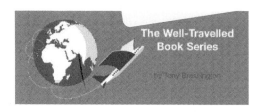

The Well-Travelled Book Series

Book 1

The Avebury Ring

by

Tony Brassington

First edition

ISBN 978-0-9569705-5-8 (Paperback)

The Well-Travelled Book Series – Book 1

Published by Tony Brassington / Mind and Achievement Ltd.

Copyright 2017 by Tony Brassington / Mind and Achievement Ltd. 2017

All Rights Reserved

Disclaimer

Please note that this book is a work of fiction, and as such all characters, business names, clubs or associations, and events are all fictitious, and have no known connection with anyone living, past or present.

My life has been forever enriched

by being married to my lovely wife,

Julie, and the blessing of our two wonderful

Daughters, Lindsey and Hayley.

Tony Brassington has a passion and knack for making the complicated much simpler to understand, so we can all gain from it. A forever practical approach and positive attitude makes Tony a "must listen to guy" in my view for everyone who wants to find out how to ... but might be afraid of looking foolish for not already knowing. Tony, thank you for your dedication and commitment to share.

Sanat Shelat – Businessman and Friend

About the Author

In 2011, after many years of dedicated study in the field of Personal Development and other related topics, I set up Mind and Achievement Ltd to help people from all walks of life to achieve their dreams and goals. Through my books, videos and seminars, I encourage people to set their minds for achievement.

www.tonybrassington.com

Introduction to the Well-Travelled Book Series

You may be the first reader of this book, which is part of The Well-Travelled Book Series, or one of its many subsequent readers, but in either case, you are now holding in your hands a very special and unique book. This is the first book of its kind to be shared and distributed in this way, and this book will be certain to have many imitators in the future, but this series of books is the original trailblazer, that led the way.

There is a very memorable line in the Johnny Depp film, *The Ninth Gate* when two antique book dealers, who are identical twins, are discussing a very rare and valuable book.

"All books have a destiny of their own, even a life of their own."

This quote encourages you think about the life of a book. The saddest thing of all for a book must be to gather dust on a shelf, never to be read, looked at, or even moved occasionally, year after year, decade after decade. There is even a Japanese word for this, Tsundoku, which defines the habit of buying books and never reading them, and then storing them with other unread books.

"There is something sad about an unread book." Thomas Hardy – *Tess of the D'Urbervilles*

The author of any book wants to believe that the time and great effort he or she put into creating their work leads to a book which is being well read in the wider world. Whilst it is true that too many books sit on shelves gathering dust, some books are indeed very well-travelled. Some books have the power to lead the reader to great life-changing discoveries and personal insights, and I would even go as far as to say that some books have a special energy of their own - the best books have a combination of all three. I would like to think that this is a book with those three qualities.

My intended purpose for this book is firstly, and just for fun, to demonstrate over time just how far and wide a book can travel around the world. Secondly, to spread a greater awareness and understanding of the Universal Laws, and, finally, to promote giving and sharing every time this book is passed along.

In order for this book to promote sharing, it should be shared, not just as a holiday book, but read and shared with other people at every opportunity. Share it with your friends and colleagues, read it and share it on a coach, bus or train, in the park, in a coffee shop, anywhere you can think of. This can add greatly to the life and adventures of the Well-Travelled Book Series as you enjoy your own life adventures.

After reading this book, please sign and date it, and then share this book with another person.

The Unexpected Departure

Chapter 1

As Simon stood in the morning sun in the open airport car park at Birmingham International Airport, he looked at the remote key fob in his hand to his newly acquired car, a Jaguar XK8 convertible. He pressed the lock button on the remote and watched with great pleasure, and an odd sense of déjà vu, as the car's various mechanisms went into action. First, the doors locked, then the windows went up, the door mirrors turned in, and the roof freed itself from the rear of the car and took up its rightful position over the vehicle, all while reflecting the summer sunlight from various, gleaming panels all painted in shiny British racing green.

With a satisfied smile and a newfound confidence in his gait, he tossed his hand luggage over his shoulder, picked up the small suitcase beside him, and headed towards the bus stop to take the short ride to the airport check-in building and to his next destination.

Contradictory to his just-recently acquired tastes, Simon had the appearance of someone who was used to the rugged outdoor life, what with his wavy, dirty-blonde, shoulder-length hair that hadn't seen a haircut in quite some time, but his lack of suntan told another story. Although he was tall and muscular, most of his handsome features were somehow hidden to the world – probably due to a poor dress sense – as he was wearing baggy shorts and the same t-shirt he'd worn at last year's London

Marathon. Simon, at 26 years of age, was a classic diamond in the rough.

The bus pulled up and Simon stepped onto it, easily manoeuvring his luggage, while he watched others struggle with theirs, as the small suitcase he carried held all of his minimal wardrobe, topped off with just a few necessities to last a ten-day holiday in his shoulder bag. It made him suddenly think of his Grandad Ted and the conversation they'd had quite a few years ago. Ted loved his teaching moments and Simon had learned quite a bit from his Grandad growing up. When Ted spoke of human beings being natural collectors, and as a result, their homes, over a lifetime, would quite resemble a museum with an assorted collection of old furniture, old clothing styles, films, music, books, and so on. Though Ted agreed that souvenirs and sentimental things could be a sign of a well-lived life, it was also a very limiting habit.

"You must always be open to the new, while loving the best of what came before," his Grandad would often say. And that was exactly what Simon was trying to do.

The car park bus made the short journey to the airport departures terminal and pulled up a short distance from the sliding doors at the front.

Simon wondered if his friends would be already inside waiting for him. As a single guy coming up to thirty, as he saw it, ten days away with some friends was something to look forward to, even if he was the odd one out amongst two couples. *They had all been friends for many years, so this odd-numbered group of five on holiday should work out okay*, he thought.

Even so, he really did want to find his perfect soul mate now, as he'd been giving a lot of thought to it these past few months. He had even tried visualisation to help speed things up a bit, but there was no sign of that helping to find his Miss Right, other than some odd recurring images that had been harassing him of late. This holiday could very well be his opportunity. Nonetheless, he was very glad to be going away, because the past few days had been nothing short of interesting for Simon Tesla Templeton; to say the least.

The double sliding doors slid apart while a small party of people in front of him entered the building. Looking over the heads of the people in front, Simon could see his friends waiting for him, just as he'd visualized. Upon seeing Simon, their faces lit up with smiles, ready to begin their holiday adventure.

"Simon," his old friend's Susan and Patrick called out fondly. The last time he'd seen them was at the London Marathon. Then, Susan had a full head of wild mahogany curls. She must have tired of the frizz, as now it was straightened to just beneath her collar bone. By her side, and carrying far too much luggage, was her husband, Scott, whom she'd married two years prior.

Patrick was sporting an overgrowth of facial hair and a bigger tummy than last year. Ah, the universal signs of a contented marriage that had outlasted a year, when previously Patrick hadn't been able to hold on to a lady for longer than a month. Petite and pretty, with porcelain-like features, Lilly complimented Patrick's robust form.

"Hey, is that the same shirt you wore last year? It is, isn't it? And I see you still haven't gotten around to a good trimming. I found where you misplaced your mop. It's on your head."

Simon was about to come back with commentary pointing out Patrick's growing middle when suddenly he was struck with a moment of dread as he realised this was another real life scene he had seen before. He began to wonder now if he would be taking this flight at all; the déjà vu that had been following him the past few days told him that he probably would not.

He recalled his dream of three night's previous. First, in the dream, he'd seen the garage forecourt across the road from his house with a beautiful, British racing green Jaguar XK8 convertible for sale on the front lot. Some might make a good case for red being the best colour for a convertible car, but Simon had thought that this particular model of Jaguar just looked fabulous in British racing green. The morning after the dream, he'd opened his bedroom curtains and looked out in total astonishment, to see a Jaguar XK8 convertible, in British racing green, for sale across the road from him - the exact same one as in his dream.

Simon got dressed and went immediately over to the garage to take a closer look, but he hadn't been able to shake that odd sense of déjà vu until he was the proud owner of that British racing green Jaguar XK8 and it was sitting in his driveway, like it was simply meant to be. The same sense of déjà vu that had made an appearance when he was in the airport car park, holding the remote key fob with its chrome leaping Jaguar emblem. Now, with the sliding doors of the airport departures entrance closing just behind him, his friends yelling to him above the crowd and looking at him and talking to him in just that way, excitedly awaiting their departure, he was now certain he recognised this unfolding scene in front of him from his same dream, which predicted that his phone would ring and lead to an abrupt change of plans.

Right on cue, his mobile phone started to ring.

Is all this really happening? he thought to himself as he took the phone out of his pocket to answer it and glanced apologetically towards his waiting friends.

"Hello Simon, my boy, it's your Grandad here, but then you already know that, don't you? You have been expecting this call from me. You must be standing in the airport check-in terminal now, about to meet up with your friends."

The smiles exchanged between Simon and his friends and their playful bantering began to lessen, as Simon's face took on a deeply concerned look. He slightly turned his back to them, saying he was having a serious conversation and something was about to change.

"I don't know how you know all that, but you must also know I am about to leave on a plane for a ten-day holiday," Simon said, trying to keep his voice quiet so his friends would not overhear.

"Sorry Simon, but you know deep down that you will not be leaving with your friends today. The recent dream you had will have told you that, although the dream only took you as far as this point today, but I can assure you that the rest of your day will be spent with me, or at least a significant part of it, as it is vitally important that we both meet and talk today."

Though Simon had always been quite fond of his Grandad, he let out a weary sigh and replied "Can't whatever this is wait until I get back?"

"I'm afraid not, Simon, we are on the Universe's time-table and schedule now. It is, in many ways, all out of my hands. You had better say goodbye to your friends and get into your green sports car and drive over to my house."

"What? – Universe? – I can't just – They're expecting me – and wait, how?" Simon struggled with his words, and then continued with some exasperation, "How do you know about my green convertible anyway? I haven't spoken with you since -" Simon put up his finger to tell Susan to give him a moment, as she'd begun walking in his direction, a worried look on her face. Patrick was tapping at the non-existent watch on his wrist to say they were running out of time.

There was a short pause, and then Grandad went on to list a few things to prove that the ball was well and truly in his court. "You had a big turning point in your life about a week ago, I know about that, too. The car that you bought two days ago is a Jaguar XK8, convertible, in British racing green. I also know that you first saw that car in a dream and you bought the car the very next day from the garage across the road from you."

Simon was very puzzled about how his Grandad could know anything about his dream or the car, as most of Simon's other family members were abroad on their holidays already, and he had not told any of them about his recent impulsive purchase, and he especially hadn't told them about the dream, or dreams, rather. As far as his big turning point, he was still just trying to figure it all out himself.

"I also know about your recurring dream of the hand and the ring," his Grandad said more quietly.

Now he really had Simon's full attention, and the serious and somewhat pained look on Simon's face told the world so.

"Ted," Simon spoke with resignation. Everyone called his Grandad, Ted, even though Ted was not his real name. No one knew, why, where, or when, it started, but, to the world, he was known as Ted. "You've got me, you win. I don't know how you know those things, but -"

"To find the answers, you must leave the airport now," Ted interrupted, as though he was the one with time restrictions, and not on the plane about to depart. Simon gestured to his friends to go ahead and board the plane and he'd join them momentarily.

"Come over to my home in Wiltshire. I will explain to you how I know about the turning point in your life. I will explain to you how I know about your Jaguar. I am certain you would be very interested to know the importance of the dream, of the woman's hand and the ring, all presented in grey, that you've been having. I can promise you that in the big scheme of things you simply must spend the rest of today with me; it's essential that you do," his Grandad insisted. "You may even meet her ...", Ted stopped short of telling Simon the details of who 'her' actually was, but clearly again, Ted knew something that Simon did not.

Simon thought Ted was talking about her, as in Miss Right, which is exactly what he'd hoped to do on his ten-day holiday with his friends. That one particular dream had been so recurring of late, and had only become more frequent since scheduling this trip with his friends. He felt it strongly and deeply inside himself, especially at Ted's mentioning of meeting her, that something profound was about to happen, and Simon was more determined than ever to go on this trip, so he spoke more assertively to his Grandad than he ever had before.

"No, I can't ... I'm very sorry, but I am going away on holiday. I am very interested to hear what you have to say and to know how you know these things about me, but there is something telling me that I have to go on this trip, and if I don't go on this trip, I will miss out on something … something I can't explain. I will come directly over to see you when I get back."

His Grandad's short pause felt like an eternity as Simon was holding his breath.

Finally, Ted replied, in a very slow and serious tone, "You're exactly right that you are meant to go on a trip, where you will fully come into your turning point and something amazing will happen, but that trip is to Wiltshire. To me. As quickly as you can get here, because, you see, Simon, I cannot wait for you to get back from your holiday with your friends, and neither should you, as I will be gone by then."

"Gone? Are you going on holiday too?"

"No Simon, my boy, by tomorrow, I will be leaving for my next adventure in time and space … I will be leaving this earth … By tomorrow, I will be dead."

Journey to Avebury

Chapter 2

Simon was soon heading back down the motorway, leaving the airport far behind him, in his Jaguar XK8 convertible, the top down and the warm summer air flowing all around him. His friends had taken the news that he would not be coming fairly well, now just two couples going on holiday without Simon being the fifth wheel.

At least it is a great day to be driving an open-top car, he thought to himself, while deriving great pleasure from the appreciative looks granted on his new ride by those passing by. He tried to relax and get himself in that positive-thinking mindset, but a number of questions and conflicting emotions kept going around in his mind.

What had just happened at the airport?

Did he really just get talked out of going on holiday with his friends?

How could his Grandad have known about the Jaguar he'd only purchased a couple of days ago; how could he have known so much about Simon's dreams, and how in the world did Ted call his mobile at the airport with such perfect timing?

"Tomorrow I will be dead." What was that all about? Especially when Ted was such a fit man.

And finally, what did Ted mean when he'd said, "You may even meet her."

All these questions and concerns filled his mind, and as the journey continued, Simon also gave some thought to where his life was at this moment in time. He did feel very lonely at times. Often he would feel incomplete, as if a big part of his being was missing. He was coming up to thirty, or at least it felt like it to him, and all his friends were paired off now. Each time he went out socially, it was with couples, and, at some point in the conversation, someone was always certain to ask, "Where is your Miss Right, Simon? Haven't you found her yet?"

He thought he had met Miss Right a couple of years ago, but unfortunately that relationship came to an unexpected end a few months ago, a loss which still hurt him very much. Glancing at the empty seat beside him, he reminisced, "That is where she should be sat now, alas."

She'd seemed quite perfect for him in almost every way, but there was one feeling Simon had never been able to shake, no matter how long he tried to do just that, and no matter how much he'd tried to convince himself otherwise. Something he couldn't articulate into words, or even coherent thoughts, had been missing or not quite right. He'd feel it most strongly those moments when he'd get a surprise look at her and feel this loss and emptiness inside himself so strongly, almost as though he was wanting her to look like something else … or someone else, rather. It had never made any sense, because she'd been extraordinarily beautiful, and those other times when she did not catch him by surprise, he had cherished looking at her.

As women can be known to pick up on things intuitively or otherwise, at times, regardless of his words of love, in the end after two years, and for the lack of an engagement ring and a wedding proposal she'd insisted that she was not the one for him.

Instead of telling her he would marry her, eventually, he'd looked at her hand and the ring he'd always envisioned, and it just didn't match up, so he'd watched her walk out the door instead, forever.

Then there were Simon's dreams and goals in life - had they ever been elusive. All the small dreams and goals had come easily enough, but the biggest ones were still as far away as ever. Simon began to wonder if Ted was about to play a significant part in bringing about some long overdue life changes in his life for the better.

Ted was correct, and Simon knew it, that there had been a turning point in Simon's life about a week ago. After Mona, Simon had made some half-hearted attempts at dating, or, more or less, his coupled-friends had attempted to set him up with this person or that. He'd thrown himself even harder into work as an Assistant Manager, completing his manager's every request, working long nights and with very little reward, watching proposal after proposal of his be rejected – not because they weren't any good, but because he could only go as far as his boss would allow him, which was beneath him.

So, after so many years of gaining more and more responsibility in work, without the reward, the pay, the title, and gradually watching his friends being paired off with their 'one', becoming homeowners, and buying and showcasing their expensive toys, Simon had thought things through and decided that enough was enough; it was time to greatly raise his game in life. He'd finally become fed up of settling for second best, fed up of living a life of watching other's win, fed up with compromise and conformity.

At the moment of realisation and commitment to this turning point, Simon had said aloud with great passion and energy, "Now it is time for me to win out with my biggest dreams and goals." After saying these words, he'd noticed how his next thought turned to finding his true soul mate in life, and that thought had directly been followed by an image from that recurring dream of his - a scene, all in grey, featuring a slender hand of a young woman with a man's hand sliding the wedding ring off her ring finger. Since the time of the turning point in Simon's life, this image from his recurring dream would now flash into his mind more often than usual, and at random times, but why?

With all these thoughts circling his mind, the time just flew away as he drove. He left one motorway and was on the next one. Travelling along the M4, he soon arrived at junction 16; his exit. After taking a few short link roads, he was on the A4361 and travelling along the beautiful, unspoilt, open countryside of Wiltshire, en route to his Grandad's house near the village of Avebury.

After city life, it was always wonderful to travel on roads surrounded by open fields. In many places in Wiltshire, it was open farmland for as far as you could see. Simon's mood began to lighten; he had so many wonderful memories of this part of the world, especially from childhood visits to Granny and Grandad. The scenery of the open countryside began to be broken up by the odd house dotted along the roadside here and there. The number of houses along the roadside increased as Simon drew nearer the village of Avebury, with its ancient stone circle.

He looked anticipatingly towards the right. "Ah, there they are," he murmured fondly as the first monolithic stone of the world-famous, ancient stone circle came into his view. The stone was known as the Diamond or Swindon Stone, which had stood in the same place for 4,500 years. This wonderful stone circle, nearly a mile across, had always caught Simon's imagination, and he continued to enjoy visiting it in his adult life. As a child, he had been lucky enough to play around this wonderful ancient monument many times.

The village of Avebury could proudly boast being surrounded by Europe's largest Neolithic stone circle, approximately 14 times larger than Stonehenge, and listed by the United Nations as a World Heritage Site. It had an earthworks surrounding it, consisting of a circular bank and ditch encompassing approximately 30 acres. The ancient stone circle site was now divided into four quadrants by its public highways, with each quadrant known by its compass position.

Simon continued past even more large monolithic stones standing tall in the fields on both sides of the road. He tipped his head at the villagers and tourists as he drove past the village pub on the right, which enjoyed a central position on the road system of Avebury village. Simon had always wondered how a village, including a pub, had ever been built right in the centre of an ancient stone circle with an earthworks surrounding it. Simon had also occasionally pondered with some amusement: if Stonehenge had been built bigger, would that too have had a village pub at the heart of it?

The Jaguar glided along the roads through Avebury and out the other side of the village, back into the open countryside until he was in view of Ted's big, modern, red brick house, with its three double garages. Large green lawns surrounded the house on every side, all with neatly mowed grass.

Simon took a few controlled deep breaths as he pulled into the wide, paved driveway to help clear his mind from all those puzzling and troubling thoughts which had kept him company throughout his journey to Avebury. Having reached his destination, he knew it was now time for a different mindset, so he pondered one final thought. On a day already full of surprises, what would the rest of this day hold and where might it lead?

For the second time that day, Simon peered at the remote key fob in his hand with great interest as to exactly how his Grandad knew about the Jaguar, and far more curiously, how his Grandad knew about Simon's dreams – a conversation he was very much looking forward to.

Ted and Simon had always got on well and they'd always had a natural rapport. Despite the strange circumstances that had led up to this visit, Simon knew it would be very enjoyable chatting with his Grandad again.

Ted always spoke like a tree. He would often branch off in different directions, but those branches were always interesting, and Ted would usually get more stirred up, passionate and animated, as the conversation went on.

Simon took a moment to admire Ted's 1972 Ford Mustang Mach 1 with twin air scoops on the bonnet. *Now that's a real American classic car,* he thought. He remembered fondly when Ted had bought this car. It was after seeing the James Bond film, *Diamonds are Forever*, though Ted had yet to drive it on two wheels as James Bond did.

"Now listen, Simon, my boy, this is a real American classic Ford. This Mustang Mach 1 has all the toys and trimmings. Great sport spec, great paint job, too, and I just love it," Ted would often say when Simon would visit from early childhood and on, perhaps influencing Simon's own appreciation for fine vehicles.

Ted had quite a diverse collection of cars, from an early classic Bentley to a modern-day Aston Martin. But that was Ted all over - a wonderful blend of the best of yesterday, while always being open to new things.

Ted possessed the same variety with his clothes, in contrast to Simon's minimal wardrobe that he'd easily fit into the small suitcase. His Grandad nearly always wore bright colours, just like his flashy cars, but you never did quite know what he'd be wearing next as he'd go from a Top Hat to a Sombrero, a sports jacket to a tracksuit top, a T-shirt to formal evening wear. It kept a youthful air about his Grandad, which is why Ted did it, without ever being too loud or over-the-top about it.

Simon wondered what he would find his Grandad wearing today as he walked around the side of the house, knowing from past experience that Ted would usually be found in his back garden or in the conservatory.

Hopefully it won't be something with any connection to his expected demise tomorrow? Simon thought with a little apprehension.

Simon entered the rear garden and found his Grandad peering at a leaf on the only shrub in the garden. He shook his head in light amusement. *That's a relief,* he thought, *it appears he chose the golfing-look today. I was afraid he might have gone for the horse jockey-look again. I'll never get that image out of my mind!*

Ted was dressed all in red: a red baseball cap, red polo shirt, and red tartan trousers. He had a small set of headphones around his neck and a CD player attached to his belt. Simon had inherited his full head of hair from his Grandad, which surprisingly, still had quite a bit of colour in it. Ted would say it was due to regularly eating the best locally-made honey with the honeycomb still in the jar.

The rear garden was all open lawns, surrounded by a very low hedge. It was a very basic garden somehow well-matched to the open rural landscape in this part of the world. The truth was that Ted was no gardener and the only shrub to be found had grown to be nearly as tall as the owner of the garden himself.

A single, round, cast-iron antique-effect garden table and two matching chairs, all painted in white, stood before this solitary plant. The table was covered with an assortment of items: a small laptop, a few books, several classical and pop music CD's, an unopened bottle of red wine with a single wine glass, and a brand new digital Dictaphone still in its box.

Next to the table, and looking quite abandoned at the moment, was a fairly large amateur telescope, easily large enough for some serious stargazing.

Simon looked briefly towards the telescope and puzzled to himself, *why does Ted have his telescope set up in his garden at this time of day? It is midday, with a bright, clear, blue sky above, but I suppose nothing should surprise me today after all that's already happened.*

Ted was so focused upon looking at a Caterpillar on a single leaf on the shrub that he did not notice that Simon was now standing a short way behind him. To get his attention, Simon made a small cough and then gently said, "You look fine to me, certainly not like someone at death's door."

Ted turned around, still somewhat distracted by the caterpillar, which had obviously captured his imagination in a big way for some unknown reason, and without any response to

Simon's words, he took his seat at the table and gestured for Simon to sit down in the opposite chair.

Simon waited patiently during those few moments of silence, waiting for Ted's mind to return to the present moment.

"Sorry, Simon, I'm back with you now. What did you say?"

"Oh, it was nothing really Ted, nothing important."

After some light, polite conversation, Simon could see that his Grandad was getting back to his normal self again, but there was still uneasiness, a type of strain in their conversation. This was very unusual for these two men, because they had always enjoyed plenty of good banter and free-flowing conversation together before.

Simon thought he would try to break the pattern of this conversation, up to now, with a bold question. "Go on then, how did a man with only hours of life left to live spend his morning?"

There was a long pause before Ted pointed to the laptop on the table and said, 'eBay'. He was looking and sounding quite guilty about something. "I spent an hour or so on eBay this morning."

"But you are a millionaire. Haven't you already got everything that you want by now?" Simon asked with some amusement.

"I have indeed."

Simon looked Ted in the eye and could see Ted's eyes revealed some mischief.

"Go on."

His Grandad's moustache tilted upward as he began to grin, which finally broke the uneasiness they'd both been feeling. "Well, for some reason, it gave me great pleasure to buy the biggest, most awkward things to deliver imaginable."

"What did you buy?" Simon chuckled.

Ted let out a responding chuckle, as he knew it was time to confess. "Well first, there was a 30 tonne, 360-degree excavator, on tracks!"

Simon's face was struggling to hold back laughter. "First? What does that mean! What more could you have possibly got?"

Ted did not want to say. They stared each other in the eye for a time; both with a smirk on their faces, and when neither of them could hold back any longer, they both fell into fits of hysterical laughter as they fully released the stress of the day up to this point and could now see the funny side of things.

"It's being delivered here in three days' time, too."

"Now fess up. What else did you get?" Simon persisted.

"No, no, no ... I can't say, I can't say. But I would like to see them deliver that excavator, though I won't be here anymore by that time."

"What were you planning to do with this 360-degree excavator anyway? Dig your own grave?" Simon played.

Both of them erupted into even more fits of laughter.

Ted turned his head to the wide expanse of open lawn, "I thought maybe I would use it in the garden, to landscape it a bit."

Simon too looked in the same direction, and then turned back to Ted, not sure if Ted was serious or not, but that bout of good laughter had allowed both of them to feel more like themselves so that Simon could now urge the conversation forward.

"Anyway Ted, let's move on. Why are we both here?"

"Good idea, Simon." Ted reached over to the new boxed-Dictaphone sitting on the table, "This is for you to keep, by the way."

While his Grandad began putting the Dictaphone together for their use, it gave Simon a few moments to look over the items on the table. Only the top CD of the music titles was clearly visible - The latest version of *The Carpenters Greatest Hits*.

There was a small pile of books all neatly stacked on top of each other with their spines displaying their titles. Again, these books were typical of Ted, a balance of old and new. Jane Austen's, *Pride and Prejudice*, James Allen's, *As a Man Thinketh*, two old books on telescopes, which both looked well-worn from regular use, a copy of *50 Success Classics* by Tom Butler-Bowdon, *Dead Men's Secrets* by Jonathan Gray, and on top of the pile was a book by the latest international best-selling author, Almondie Shampine.

This book must represent the something-new, Simon thought to himself, and it had a bookmark indicating that Ted had already read well over half the book.

"I see you are reading Almondie Shampine now," Simon commented, trying to carry forth the conversation.

Ted was quite engrossed with the difficulty he was having trying to fit the batteries into the new Dictaphone, but eventually he replied, "Almondie Shampine, there is someone who knows what she wants in life, and she keeps on going after it no matter what life throws at her, or how little support she receives from others. I recently heard Almondie giving an interview on the radio about the struggles early in her career to get published as a writer, but look at her now. I approve of people like that who keep on until they get the result they desire, don't you? So I bought one of her books. To be very honest, I have been enjoying it, but as things have turned out, I suspect I will not be able to finish it in time now. Maybe I'll read one more chapter later on today, before I go. That would be nice."

When Ted finally had the new Dictaphone ready for use, and was feeling somewhat accomplished for mastering this small device, he pressed the record button and proudly said, "There we are Simon, my boy, we're in business. Now, I bet you would like a few answers as to how we have both ended up here today. I am truly sorry that you had to miss your holiday, by the way, but I promise you that in a few days' time you will be very glad that you did."

Ted placed the Dictaphone in the centre of the table. "I am recording our chat on this Dictaphone for you to keep for posterity. As these may well be some of the last words I speak here on Earth, and the fact that no one will believe you about some of the things I am about to tell you – predictions and such – without hearing it from me themselves.

"Also, the conversation I am about to have with you will cover a lot of ground in a short period of time. Recording our conversation will be better than any amount of note-taking, or trying to remember it all. In this way, you can play it over and over again in the future to review it. The new person about to enter your life will find it equally interesting and relevant to her also."

Simon's eyebrows rose up slightly at the mention of this unknown new person about to enter his life. He was full of questions, full of curiosity, but he knew this was his Grandad's way of preparing for another of his infamous teaching moments, so he continued to wait patiently, though this day was quite a bit unusual, and Ted was taking a bit longer than normal, as though he was reluctant to share what he knew and, more importantly, how he knew such things that he should not have known.

As though Ted had read Simon's ever-pondering mind, he squinted at Simon with animated eyes and said, "Our phone conversation earlier today, when you were walking into the airport - that must have all been a real surprise, eh?" He chuckled for one last measure, then finally sat back in his chair and looked at Simon with a level-head. Finally, it was time.

"I will tell you how I know the things I do. I will explain to you some more about the deeper meanings of that dream of yours - the one with the hands and the ring - and for good measure, I will give you some success tips that will last a lifetime, if you remember them and apply them, as I am certain you will. On that last point, it is an odd human trait that the things we get for nothing, we do not appreciate. You have paid a price to be here with me today, the price of missing your holiday, so you will never forget the rich content of our conversation, or fail to apply it."

Then Ted let out an abrupt sigh that alarmed Simon, and a moment's silence passed. "What I am about to tell you is a secret I have kept to myself for quite a long time, except for a few who privately shared with me their own similar experiences. I certainly never spoke of this before with any of my family members, so you will be the first, Simon, my boy, as I believe you may have the same gift, and I would like to teach you how to understand it and apply it before I go."

"Gift? What sort of gift could you possibly be talking about, Ted?" Simon was growing more and more weary with his Grandad's references to his passing.

"I do not want to go too deeply into this, so here are the basics. As a child, I used to be able to do this thing. Even now, I am not sure what the correct word is, or the correct term to describe it would be. I would imagine the term out-of-body-experience comes the closest. Anyway, whatever the correct word or term is, I could do it. I would leave my body when I was a child and fly off to distant places. Usually this would happen as I slept at night, but occasionally, if I dozed off during the day, it might happen then too.

"And when I say fly off to distant places, I mean that I would really travel afar. Not just around this world, but all over our solar system and beyond. Back then, when I was a child, my favourite place was the Moon. To a young kid, the Moon was a fantastic playground. I would tell my Mom and Dad about all the amazing things I had seen up there. There are all these ancient, derelict buildings up there, and so much more. It really is such a fascinating place."

Ted's face looked animated and almost youthful as his eyes looked afar in his retelling of his fond memories of this period in time. "My Mom and Dad would listen to me talking about what I had seen up there, and then pat me on the head and say, 'That's nice, son.' Alas, as I started to grow and mature, they really did not like to hear me talking about that kind of thing at all anymore. They considered it a bit odd. That is when I realised that it was a secret that I should not share with others. A pity, because I continued to have so many amazing experiences."

Ted's face contorted into a type of gloominess, "Then one day, it just stopped. I just couldn't do it anymore. A few other people have told me that they too had similar experiences of being able to leave their body for a time, when they were very young. I think it must be something to do with the development of the brain. Adult brains really are no fun," he said with genuine disappointment, and all of a sudden, he looked very tired and beat.

Simon's alarm and weariness turned to deep concern, and, for the first time today, he began to wonder about his Grandad's health, mainly that of his mind. It had always been a usual thing for Ted to go places in his mind. He'd become engrossed or distracted by something, such as earlier with the caterpillar; his eyes would take on a glazed, distant look, like he was somewhere else, but then he'd return and be back to himself again. This time was different. Ted's mind was wandering far more than usual, then to be talking about playing on the moon like he had actually been there.

Simon touched his Grandad's hand in an effort to bring him back to the present, though that type of affection was rare, almost unheard of, with the two. "I would go places when I was a child too, Ted, especially when I was dreaming or daydreaming. I still like to dabble in those sorts of things from time to time. Daydreaming, that is."

"So, you see, Simon, you do have the gift," Ted said excitedly. "It's not often that I am wrong about such things, I do say."

"I would dream of going on all these great adventures and doing all these admirable things. I'd have superpowers and unmatched strength. Then after seeing the Peter Pan movie for the first time, I used to daydream that I could fly to Never Never Land."

Ted's face drooped, his excitement being abruptly stolen from him.

"These were all just dreams and fantasies that my mind ran away with, Ted. I didn't actually go to such places. It was, I guess you could say, all in good fun."

Ted pulled at his moustache speculatively, as Simon knew he would do when frustrated, but not something he'd done since Simon had grown away from the child that may not have always been so open to Grandad's lengthy teaching moments, when there were much more fun things to do.

"Yes, yes, Simon, I do see the point you are trying to make and I do understand why you would think such a thing. Mom and Dad would say the same thing, so let me just say this to you, Simon, my no-fun-adult-brain-grandson. If what I'm saying to you wasn't true, then how should I know about your British racing green Jaguar, your dreams, especially the recurring one, and how is it that you could know about purchasing that fine car before you even saw it, or how could you know that I would call when I did? And mostly, how would I know that you would know that I would call? That is far more than simply dreaming and playing out little imaginary fantasies, don't you think?"

Ted let Simon ponder this for a moment before he said, "Are you ready to truly listen now, Simon? If things are to align correctly, we really don't have all that much time, especially with all that I need to share with you before I go."

"So I really did go to Never Never Land, is that what you are trying to tell me, Ted?" Simon said with a grin.

And they both burst out laughing, ready to begin again.

Ted's Table

Chapter 3

"Now that I have your full attention, Simon, though a touch of scepticism is to be expected, I was very pleased to have this rare skill come back to me a week ago, but for one night only. Again, I could move freely around without my physical body. This time, though, I had a different experience altogether - an experience I did not have during my childhood out-of-body experiences.

"As I started to soar above the Earth, I experienced what I can only describe as an overview of the Universe, a glimpse of eternity, a great knowledge. Again, I am really not sure how to put it into words. It is very hard to describe something that is, by its very nature, beyond human words or understanding. All a person can do is to greatly simplify the experience in order to describe it.

"While up there, I was on my own; there was no Spirit Guide or Supreme Being or anything like that. It was just me, but I could see everything. I became aware of a great knowledge so vast and detailed, of the past, the present, and the future. I could see the full workings of the Universal Law of Cause and Effect, as it worked its way through the many lifetimes of so many people. Oh, how we wrong each other and ourselves too," Ted pondered with some consideration. "One single step changes the course of events and the future for everyone, so the future is forever changing, at times evolving, other times regressing to repeat history, cycling through the births and deaths and lives of so many.

"Unfortunately, no human mind can retain that amount of information and knowledge when the soul is back in its human form. Of everything I saw up there that night, only the smallest fragments of it remain now, mostly just those things relevant to the lives of three people- you, me, and her. I think the Universe may have called on me to use me for one of its many grand designs before I go."

"Her?" Simon enquired, as Ted lingered on a long pause.

"Her, the her that I speak of is ..." Ted leaned towards Simon and spoke slowly and softly. "The her that I speak of is connected to that recurring dream of yours. Please forgive me, but let me describe to you what you see in that dream of yours."

Simon both looked and felt uneasy. It was one thing to go along with those that claimed they had 'special abilities'. It was a whole other thing to witness something which seemed so unrealistic and impossible, such as his Grandad recounting his very private dreams that he'd never spoken of.

"It's all right, Simon" Ted said reassuringly before continuing to speak softly and respectfully, "There are two scenes you see in this recurring dream of yours. The first scene is all in grey. There is a young woman's hand with her fingers out-stretched; her hand and wrist are all that can be seen of her. On one finger, she is wearing a wedding ring. Though her hand is youthful and beautiful, as she must also be, it is also icy-cold and lifeless. You are also in that dream too, aren't you, Simon? There is a man's hand coming into view; it's your hand, and it is your hand that removes her wedding ring."

Simon looked quite pained by this. The thought of him being a player in this dream had always troubled him. Seeing himself removing a ring from a lifeless, feminine hand had always been quite unsettling, but he maintained his composure.

"You are correct again, Ted, and I am sure beyond any doubt that you also know the second scene from this dream too, so why don't I tell it? In the second scene there is a storm, and it is raining quite heavily with the daylight falling fast. I am also in this second scene of the dream. I am kneeling in front of what appears to be a gravestone. With my hands, I am trying to dig a small hole, but the hole I am digging is filling up with rain water as fast as I try to dig out the earth.

"Around me, the growing darkness is occasionally lit by a flash of lightening, soon followed by the rumbles and loud cracks of thunder, but still I dig away frantically, completely focused on my task. When I have dug about half an arm's length or maybe more, I put a gold ring in the hole I have dug and fill it back in with the watery mud, which is now all around me."

Ted nodded in agreement, "That is pretty much how I would have told it too."

"I can tell you now, Ted, in all honesty, that these two scenes have tormented me and haunted me all my life, which is why I have never talked about this dream before with anyone. Somehow, it feels like a release to do so, to get it off my chest a bit. The ring would appear to be the only connection between these two scenes in my dream, but what does it all mean? What is this dream trying to tell me? Am I some kind of Robin Hood grave robber, or something?

"When I had the dream of the Jaguar, it was obviously a futuristic dream, as when I awoke, that same Jaguar had suddenly appeared for sale across the street. Then there was all the déjà vu I kept feeling from the moment I woke up, drove to the airport, intending on going on holiday with my old friends, all the while knowing I would get a phone call that would disrupt my plans. I have been having that recurring dream more often than ever before. Does that mean that these two scenes that I've been dreaming are about to occur?" Simon said with some nervous energy.

"Simon, I have to tell you something very important, something that you will need to know in order to make any sense of this recurring dream, so that you can then move forward with your life. It is actually not a dream at all! In fact, the scenes you see are of strong memories from a past life."

Simon looked a little shocked before exclaiming "Memories from a past life? I don't think so."

"Let's just back up a bit and add a bit more detail," Ted returned to his normal flow of speech. "As I said previously, after my out-of-body experience a few nights back, when I returned to Earth, I returned with a great deal of knowledge that I did not have before. Much of this knowledge directly relates to the lives of you, me and her. Timing is everything and we each have our own separate part to play to ensure that you and her meet up at exactly the right time and place.

"That is why when my soul returned to its human body, I knew when you would be entering the airport, I knew about that turning point of yours a few days ago and the wheels that turning point has put into motion. I was shown your Jaguar and the dreams of the hand and the ring. I was shown all of that in order to get your full attention when I called you at the airport, and also to assist you from this point forward. I am even in possession of quite a lot of detail relating to my own final hours here on Earth, and even that knowledge was given to me to help ensure that you two would both meet at exactly the right time, and in exactly the right place.

"I can give you a term which will best describe the importance of why you two must meet. By telling you this term, you will see why it is so important that you are here with me now and not flying off to the sun on your holiday."

Ted paused for a moment, straightened, and looked Simon directly in the eye, "Simon, the her that I keep referencing is your eternal soul mate and you are very close to meeting her. When you two finally meet up again, this time around, without any doubt, it will be something more than just love at first sight for both of you. It will be one of the most special and amazing moments of your lives. I am not talking about a once-in-a-lifetime moment here. This moment in time, and especially this time around, that you will both share together will be something so unique and special that, in truth, it would be more accurately described as a once-in-many-lifetimes' moment. How special is that? You see, both of you are more than just soul mates.

"You are and always have been eternal soul mates, which means that you have always ended up together in so many shared lifetimes, sharing a great many adventures in time and space. It is not just a figure of speech in your case. She really is, quite literally, your eternal and true, one and only, soul mate, which the Universe designed for you. Each human being possesses an eternal soul which returns to Earth and other realms too, living out so many lives and experiencing so much throughout these lives. Our souls must learn and grow, evolving throughout so many lifetimes and experiences."

Ted leaned back in his chair and placed his finger upon his chin as he would do when he was getting comfortable with explaining a certain subject matter, "I know not everyone wants to believe in reincarnation and the idea that we keep coming back, but let me share an opinion of mine with you, for what it's worth. It is not necessarily right or wrong; it is just an opinion based on my interpretation of all that I have seen and heard on this subject over a lifetime. If we are really honest about it, no one knows for certain where we go after death. In truth, on this particular very important subject, there are only historical stories, opinions and beliefs, all mixed in with some very human distortions of any real facts, as well as the odd bit of discreet political manipulation throughout the centuries too - quite a lot of it, in fact.

"As for history, well, that is very far from accurate. History is so shot full of holes it makes a colander look watertight. However, when you really think about it with an open mind, the only opinion that should carry any weight, and that anyone should actually listen to and consider on this important topic, is from the people who have been there. I'm talking about those people who have died on the operating table, for example. They may have been technically dead for 30 minutes or so, and then the doctor brought them back to life.

"When someone like that comes back to life and they start to talk about their experience of leaving their body and floating up the tunnel of life, and then they describe all they have seen on the other side, surely that must carry some weight. Because they are not talking theory, they are talking about their actual experience! Then there is a second equally-important group of, shall we say, expert witnesses. Many Psychiatrists have reported many interesting cases, thousands of them, in fact, of their clients talking about their past lives under hypnosis. There are so many great books on this subject, not written by cranks, rather educated people whom have spent decades of their professional lives studying this field. In both cases, be it an out-of-body experience, or hypnosis, reincarnation is often a very strong, recurring theme."

Simon looked a little uneasy. Ted had just given him quite a bit of information in a short space of time; it was a lot to take in. "I can see how an out-of-body experience could lead to the insights you clearly possess at the moment. You certainly have a view of the bigger picture which the rest of us do not. I am not sure about reincarnation, though. It is not something my religion endorses. But, love at first sight at an advanced level; yes, I would have some of that," Simon grinned.

Ted let out a slight chuckle, as if to acknowledge that the 'cat was out of the bag'. "I know all of that is a lot to take in, isn't it Simon? I would just like to add, and I admit it might sound like a contradiction, but I am not taking anything away from anyone's religious beliefs, or the value and benefit they personally gain from their religion, but the fact remains, you will meet her very soon and everything I have told you will present itself.

"The girl in your dream really is your true eternal soul mate. There is a tight window of opportunity, and you really do not want to miss it. You must remember that everything you seek is also seeking you, as your soul mate is also right now seeking you. The Universe gave you a dream a few nights ago - the Jaguar, the airport, and a series of unfolding events; of which you being here with me now is a result. Think about it in terms of the Universal Law of Cause and Effect.

"In other words, you are in the right place at the right time because the Universe left a series of clues. Clues that you followed and have led you here, and will also lead you to a point in time where you will both meet. Paradoxically, the Universe has gone to great lengths to get you to this point in time. Not just by its own designs and involving myself in such, but because of your own thoughts - the thoughts that you have sent out to the Universe - again, cause and effect.

"The Universe will find ways to show your soul mate how to be in the right place at the right time. She too will have her series of unfolding events. One way or another, she will be in the right place at the right time and so will you. Even as we speak, she is looking for you. Just as you have been looking for her, by wanting an end to the loneliness you are feeling at the moment combined with the energy you released at that turning point of yours a few days back.

"Whatever you seek is also seeking you, which is a key factor in the Universal Law of Attraction. Too many people do not understand just how important it is to direct their thoughts only to the things they wish to have in their lives. Thoughts are the cause, and life is the effect."

"So, do you think that I am going to meet this soul mate of mine in Wiltshire?" Simon asked curiously.

"I know that you will. As I have said, I know quite a good number of details relating to the part that I play in my final hours and you meeting up with your eternal soul mate."

On hearing Ted talk about his final hours, Simon looked a little amused by this, still not willing to believe for one moment that Ted was anywhere near his end.

Ted continued, "I can only give you some very basic details. If I were to tell you too much, I would be interfering with the natural flow of unfolding events and the timetable of the Universe. If you were both to rush ahead and take some short cuts, sure, you would still meet, but there is a real danger that you would both miss an important moment in time, which connects your past lives with your present ones. You know, sometimes we humans need to feel a little lost and confused by events. Too many people let this get them down, when, in reality, they should see it for what it is - an opportunity to think things through and discover a new way forward.

"You two will meet in Wiltshire, and why not? Wiltshire and its surrounding counties are all very special areas of England and always have been, for all kinds of reasons. Maybe I should use the old English term, Wessex, to better describe this part of England, as the Victorian author, Thomas Hardy, would have done. He lived in the neighbouring County of Dorset, and he very much appreciated and understood the uniqueness of his own county and its neighbouring counties. Many people believe that there is a special energy released in some parts of Wessex, because this living planet of ours releases her energy at a number of ancient energy hotspots. But it is more than simply just that. For thousands of years, this part of England has been very unique in many different ways. The evidence is all around us.

"Look at the wonderful city of Bath, for example. In the time of the Romans, Bath had the only naturally heated spring water baths in the world. Presumably, you would nearly always receive a cold bath elsewhere in the world at that time, unless you paid the high price of having your water heated on an open fire for you. Look at Stonehenge, which is only a few miles away from here, and we have Glastonbury too; what an amazing place that is, with the Glastonbury Tor visible for miles around."

Simon nodded in agreement, and then added, "Yes, the Tor sitting on top of the hill at Glastonbury is quite something. The remains of a church, otherwise known as St Michael's Tower, a church tower without a roof. Uniquely, all four sides of the tower are all different from each other, and St Michael's Tower is something of a mystery, too, for in many ways, even today, much of its early history remains unknown. But there you are, the Tor and the hill it sits on are both prominent features of the landscape which can easily be seen for miles."

"Right, Simon, my boy," Ted said, growing more and more animated. "This whole area is just full of so many ancient stones and earthworks. Some of the stones in this part of the World are older than the stones used in the Egyptian pyramids. We are not short of great caves around here, too. Wookey Hole and the Cheddar Caves, for example, both attract thousands of visitors each year. That's only to name a few features of Wiltshire and its surrounding counties, but my favourite place is right here. I have been so lucky to have lived here for decades next to the village of Avebury with its wonderful ancient stone circle. Up until three years ago, your Gran was here with me too. A lifetime well spent."

Ted became reflective for a moment and then his thoughts returned to the Avebury stones. "A few centuries ago, some damn fool thought it was a good idea to bury most of them, the stones, I mean. In came the new religion of the time, Christianity, then they literally tried to bury the past. Nothing new in that, how history repeats itself, even today. Back then they would dig a very big hole in the ground directly in front of these stones and simply push the stone into it.

"Today, there are more stones still under the ground down there in the village than there are stones standing above it. I suspect they would have buried every single stone back then if they could. If it hadn't been for one poor soul becoming trapped under one as it fell, they probably would have, too. That guy was buried alive and crushed to death at the same time, no messing. I think after that happened, people lost interest in digging away under such big stones, so the last ones have remained standing.

"It makes you wonder, though, just exactly what else they may have completely buried, wiped out of sight - quite a lot, I suspect. Anyway, Avebury was lucky, and over the years a good number of stones have been saved and raised back up to their rightful place above ground. I really hope that one day they will all be raised back up.

"Should I have had more time, I may have been able to put my newly-purchased excavator to good use. That would have been quite fun, don't you think, Simon? Your old Grandad restoring all the stones above ground, making a name for myself in history. I don't know what those stones meant to the people of ancient times, but now, in this day and age, I think they have a new connection with people, something they cannot find anywhere else. There's a small team of Archaeologist's digging down there in the Avebury stone circle at this very moment."

"That sure would have been something to see, Ted. But I couldn't possibly imagine what you would wear sitting high up in your big excavator, digging up those stones," Simon chuckled.

Briefly, Ted recalled a memory and then chuckled a bit himself, "I bet you don't remember that time when you were a toddler. It was your first visit to the stone circle. You could not be drawn away from one of stones, one of the original stones as I recall, one which had never been buried. Somehow that ancient monolithic stone must have really meant something to you."

"Do you remember which stone it was?"

"Sorry, Simon, it was years ago. I don't remember now."

"I bet you do," Simon replied with a smile, sparring with Ted just a little. Ted sat back in his chair and tilted his head for a moment. As he did this, Simon couldn't help but notice the knowing glint in Ted's eye, saying he knew perfectly well which stone it was, so why wasn't he telling?

Before Simon could quiz Ted any more on this topic, Ted firmly announced, "Let's move on to the topic of your turning point. We have so much to get through and so little time."

The Three Steps to

Destination Success

Chapter 4

"Turning points, now Simon, that is an interesting topic. Yours came to you a few days ago, though it had been building inside of you for quite some time. Turning points are something everyone should be talking about and aware of what they mean, yet nobody appears to ever mention them. Occasionally, you might read about one in a good biography, or the odd rare interview, but that's it.

"That is the great tragedy of mankind. Here we are the most privileged form of life on the planet - it is our show, our party. Forgive me for being blunt, but despite this great privilege our species enjoys, the average person is pretty much asleep to their true potential. Hell, take a look at any one of the real experts in the field of human-potential, the speakers and writers who do not attempt to whitewash the subject. They usually all start from this key point.

"Most people are sleepwalking their way through the years. They follow the crowd without any trace of real independent thought. I would like to say there should be a turning point in everyone's life. There should be, but there usually isn't any sign of one. For most, life is an imponderable mystery. Something they never take the time to figure out or take the time to think through properly. We have free will, we have free choice, yet this great gift appears to count for nothing."

"Hey Ted, come on, that is pretty strong stuff. I'd hardly call mine a turning point – more just fed up with the same thing and never seeming to go any further than where I'm at, like walking on a conveyor belt moving in the opposite direction as me. I imagine everyone must feel that way from time to time."

"Ah, you see, but here is where I make my point, Simon. Just because someone may feel something does not mean that it will lead to thoughts that will then result in action. Most will disregard the feeling and not give it a second's thought, other than, perhaps, to think that there isn't a thing in the world they can do about it, so then they just carry forth as is. Also remember that all of us are eternal souls here on earth in physical form."

Ted paused for a moment to consider his direction of thought, "Let's focus on you. That is the reason why we are here. This is the second time in your life when you have had a turning point. A turning point begins with a moment in time when you really think about the path you are presently on and where it will ultimately lead to.

"On two occasions, you have been big enough to say, 'I do not want this', and then you thought about what you truly wanted in your life and you then committed yourself to it. As you applied this commitment, a whole series of subtle, and some not-so-subtle, changes and events soon took place. You arranged the holiday with your friends, scheduled two weeks off of work to attempt to find what you're seeking, purchased the Jaguar, and now here you are."

"I seem to recall someone quite persistently insisting I come here instead of going on holiday with my friends. Then, when I was more determined than before to have this vacation, someone using the old guilt-trap of telling me that I may never see them again," Simon smirked with light amusement, goading his Grandad into perhaps sharing more of his enlightened experiences, such as his seeming awareness of his final hours on earth when Ted was as fit as a fiddle, or just revealing where this eternal love of Simon's was.

Ted ignored him with that same knowing glint in his eye. "You see, Simon, any fool can be unhappy with their lot in life and complain about it. That alone counts for nothing. A person must choose a new direction, an aim in life, or best of all, set a big goal for themselves. Those are the first two of the three stages or steps of a turning point. To reject the path you are presently on, and then choose something new."

"Two of three? You must tell me about the third, because the first turning point of mine that you speak of was when I was in my teens when I walked out of an apprenticeship and went into business for myself. Alas, my business folded after a year."

"But Simon, look at all you achieved in that year! Yes, the market changed and this meant the closure of your unique single-product business, but you made, and banked, more money in that one year than most people do after a whole lifetime of hard work. Come on, I am certain you paid for that Jaguar in full, no cash loans for you."

"Well, maybe you are right about that one, Ted. That is the most I have spent so far of the money I made from that year."

"I was so proud of you for what you achieved back then, especially in such a short period of time. You were so young, yet you served your customers well and were honest with them all."

"Yes, I made a nice bit of cash back then, which I saved for a rainy day, or to use for a new business, but so far I have not come across the right new venture for me. Unfortunately, because I did not have a clear new business direction back then, I drifted into a number of dead end jobs. After a few years of that, it sort of takes the shine of the good times, and life too, to some extent. You spoke of those who drift through life, and it may very well just be the disappointment of failure or the fear of such that keeps people just accepting their life as is and not moving forward from it."

"Well Simon, luckily for you, you have found your motivation again. You thought things through again and have arrived at a second turning point in your life. You decided that enough is enough and it is time to greatly raise your game in life once again. Understandably, you are fed up of settling for second best, fed up of living a life of watching others win, and fed up with compromise and conformity."

Simon almost balked at hearing Ted's words practically verbatim to Simon's own thoughts that preceded his turning point. His Grandad's tales were becoming more and more believable the more he spoke.

"Do you know what I personally like best about turning points? When you truly commit to a new direction or change in your life, the Universe puts many wheels in motion on your behalf, more than you'll ever know," Ted said, as though reading Simon's thoughts. "Turning points usher in a whole series of changes. For example, you bought the Jaguar because your whole self-image has changed as a result of your turning point."

Simon suddenly felt a renewed energy within him, "That is true, and my shoulder-length hair is going to change as well. It is time for a hairstyle more in keeping with my new self-image. My long hair seemed right for the old me, but not the new. Now it is time for me to win out and achieve my biggest dreams and goals, and according to you, my soul mate, who is just around the bend. So, how about I get to that?" He became smug.

"Recall, just moments ago, when I spoke of cutting corners. Simon, to complete this new turning point in your life and to make it count, you must have a complete understanding of the third step of a turning point, and that is what you intend to GIVE!"

Humbled, Simon returned to getting comfortable in his chair for the remainder of their conversation. "What I intend to give? Wait a minute, you said in a turning point you first reject the old, then choose something new, or in other words - set a new goal. Goal setting is about gaining something, not giving something away."

"Simon, it is vitally important to learn, master, and apply this third turning point stage. It makes all the difference in the world, not just in terms of achieving your goal, but equally as important, is holding on to it once you have achieved it. Most important of all, or the real trick, if you like, is, you must know what it is you intend to give. Only then will you truly succeed.

"This is the reason so many fail. They think all you need to do is decide what it is that they want, and then call it a goal and a good job done. Nothing is further from the truth. They have no understanding of the Laws of the Universe. There has to be balance. In order to receive, first, you must give. It is something so simple and basic, yet almost everyone misses this vital point.

"Think of it another way. A convict doing time for robbery knew what he wanted and took it, but his giving to restore the balance has to be paid back in time. There are many methods one can choose to apply the giving. Sometimes the product will do all the giving because it directly helps people, or it solves a problem for people. It can be to give better service or better quality than any of your competitors. Occasionally, it is to give something back directly to society, such as through charitable donations, but no matter how you do it, give you must.

"I can tell you, in all honesty, that I did not make any real progress in my business and private life until I began to understand the importance of the giving side of the equation. When I understood it, I very soon went from strength to strength in all areas of life. Now look at me, am I not an example of someone who has gone from rags to riches?"

"Actually, when you think about it, it makes perfect sense to me. Over the years, I have heard many successful people say things like, 'I like to give something back', and they are nearly always in the highest leagues of success. On that point of great successes and giving, what did you give, Ted?"

"Simon, my boy, isn't it obvious?" Ted whole-heartedly laughed. "Did you really think that all this time I talk just to hear myself talk?"

"Your teaching moments," Simon said with awe.

"You are, by far, not the only one that has had to sit here and listen to me impart my wisdom and knowledge onto, whether you wanted it or not. In fact, right before you arrived today, I had another visitor come seeking advice."

"Who?"

Ted then thought twice about revealing who this visitor was, so he continued to explain his point while pretending not to have heard Simon's question. "So now you appear to understand the importance of giving - the third stage of a turning point. Some people I can think of would never get that point, but neither can I imagine them as very successful people either. Getting back to you and your turning point, Simon, part one, which is typically the hardest step for most people, rejecting your old course, is completed. Part two, choosing something new. Forgive me for saying it, but it is still very general for you at the moment; you will need to spend some time thinking this through in greater detail and refining it. As for step three, you also really need to think this through, do some soul-searching, and align it with your step two. It will be the giving that will deliver to you your chosen step two. If you take the time to seriously think through these three steps, I promise you, success will soon come your way."

Ted started to look excited and pleased as he said, "After all, that's where the Universal Laws of Thinking come into play, which I'm really looking forward to explaining to you, but first, there is one other good piece of advice I would like to share with you, and in many ways, it actually connects well with step three of your turning point."

Ted reached over to the pile of compact discs on the table and picked up *The Carpenters Greatest Hits* CD. Holding it in his hand, he said, "Don't follow the crowd. To follow the crowd is folly." Then he tapped on the cover of the CD case and said, "These two know what I am talking about - Richard and Karen Carpenter. They did things their way, which meant they stood out from the crowd. You know nowadays all the so-called success experts are advising everyone to emulate someone else. What a load of hogwash, a sure road to nowhere fast, or certainly the back of the queue behind all of the other emulators.

"They say that if you are failing, find someone who appears not to be failing, and copy, or emulate, what they are doing." Ted offered up both hands in puzzlement. "That is like success education for ten-year-olds. Why do adults buy into that sort of wholesale nonsense? Why can't people think bigger than that? Let me give you an example or two. Over the years, I have heard a few male singers described as the next *Frank Sinatra,* or some other big singing star. That is usually the kiss of death for them and their career. Occasionally they might make the odd album or two, but they don't enjoy anything like the success of the star they are being compared to.

"It is the same thing for authors. How many writers have we heard being compared at some time to J.K. Rowling, Stephen King, Jules Verne, Agatha Christie, or whoever it might be. I say thanks, but no thanks. I didn't get to where I got in life by following the strategies of others. The big point that everyone is missing is, to emulate another person is only good up to a point, but there comes a time to be yourself. The first and best original you. Let others emulate you!"

Ted tapped *The Carpenter's* CD case again. "As I said, these two did things their way and enjoyed great success as a result. Yes, I know I'm an old guy, and their time on the pop music scene was years back, but The Carpenters still serve as a great example of the point I am trying to make. So please listen to me well. I was lucky enough to catch them being interviewed on the radio many years ago when I was over in the USA for a time. The theme of the interview was their new Album called *Passage* - another great example of the work and unique style of Richard and Karen Carpenter. I could talk for hours about what makes their music so special, so please do not ask me to explain that to you, or we will never finish our chat.

"Anyway, both Karen and Richard were asked various questions throughout the interview, but I will never forget two answers Richard Carpenter gave. I can recall them even now, word for word; let me quote Richard - 'You can't go into a recording studio and worry about what everybody on the outside is thinking.', and 'An artist has to do what they feel suits them best, and what they like best. That is the foremost thing. Not whether it is going to sell or please the critics ... It has to please the artist or you are selling out.'"

Ted placed the CD case gently down on the table and then he asked Simon, "Can you see just how much success-wisdom lies within those quoted lines? I tell you, I have thought about those lines over and over many times in my life and look at me. Did I follow the crowd? No I didn't, thanks to hearing that interview. I urge you to do the same, be yourself - your best self. Stand out from the crowd by doing things your way. Most important of all, when it comes to the giving step of your turning point, think about those two quotes and do things your way. Let others follow the crowd. The world does not need more of the same. It has enough, but it is always ready for something new and it is always ready for something better."

Ted paused for a moment, as if to underline the point he had just made, and then he clapped his hands and rubbed them together with enthusiasm, in readiness for delivering his next few words of wisdom.

"I see you love talking about this stuff, don't you, Ted?" Simon smiled. He was enjoying the conversation, some of which he had heard from Ted before, but this time there were a few new ideas, which could help to make a whole world of difference in Simon's new endeavours.

"I do indeed. Which brings me on to the Laws of Thinking - well, almost. But first, let's talk about Toyota."

"Toyota?" Simon questioned with light amusement. Ted and his many, many branches to his talking tree.

"Yes, that's right. Toyota Land Cruiser, in fact. Years ago, when four-wheel drive vehicles were not built as well and as reliable as they are today, the Australians had a saying, 'If you want to explore the outback, you'll need a four-wheel drive. If you want to come back alive, you'll need a Toyota Land Cruiser!' Only two sentences, but if you were planning to explore the outback at that time, don't you think the second sentence is vitally important to know and thoroughly understand? The complete quote is loaded with very important information, to be ignored at your peril.

"That is how it is with advice from other people and very often from experts, too. They're missing the important pieces that tell the whole story. Which brings me to the point I want to impress upon you as you will find it to be a real game changer. Countless so-called success experts and Gurus retell a very valuable quote, 'If you keep doing the same things, you will keep getting the same results.' And, of course, they are right. It is madness to expect anything else, yet people do.

"I realised some years ago that this quote is actually only half the story, and like the Toyota Land Cruiser quote, adding another line completes it. The quote should be, 'If you keep thinking the same things, then you will keep doing the same things, which will always lead to the same results.' Your *results* in life are a direct reflection of your *actions*, your actions are a direct result of your *thinking* or thoughts. It is not simply knowing what everyone else knows - it's knowing that bit more, which puts you at a real advantage. The real advantage in life is to know the Laws of the Universe, especially the Laws of Thinking."

Simon nodded in agreement, "That is an interesting point. It makes a lot of sense, too. It is a peculiar thing with memory that often we need a mental hook to help remember things, and the Toyota Land Cruiser provides one very nicely."

"So true Simon, it really baffles me when I think about it, that first we need to remember something else before the actual thing we want to remember. Why is it that we so often need a mental hook to remember things, instead of simply being able to recall the information as is? Read any book on improving memory and that mental hook tip will always be in it."

"Laws of Thinking, you were about to say –"

"Oh yes, let's not digress. Earl Nightingale really had this covered in his audio recording, The Strangest Secret. To quote Earl's words, you will 'become what you think about.' And there you are, everything summed up in one sentence.

"There is, of course, much more to be learned on the subject of the Laws of Thinking, but it is an excellent starting point. Each thought is a seed in the garden of the mind, and, as Earl pointed out in The Strangest Secret, the mind, just like the soil in your garden, does not care what is planted in it, but it will return what is planted in it. Good or bad, mind or garden, if you plant it, then you own it, although life's cry-babies will always complain that life's not fair. The fact remains that at any point in time a new seed can be planted in the garden of the mind and will ultimately be harvested.

"That is what happens with a turning point - the old growing crop is uprooted and new seeds are planted. Whether it is a long, lingering thought that has been held for a very long period of time, or a strong heat-of-the-moment thought, both are thought seeds. The Laws of Thinking requires that each person develop their ability to think deeply for themselves, and that process begins by going deep into your mind and taking a look at what is in there. Take the time to meditate, reflect, even to daydream, to get the imagination working again.

"You know, Simon, if the average person said what they were thinking, the silence would be deafening. To get the best out of the Laws of Thinking, we all must get real clarity of thought. We must question where our ideas, beliefs, and opinions come from. Are they based in truth or facts? If a person has a strong opinion on something, but after some reflection and soul-searching they find that opinion is based on nothing more than what their friends or family also believe, then they really must question it and be open-minded enough to look for the real truth.

"We each absorb many influences in life through the Laws of Thinking. Your parents knew that some of those influences would be good and beneficial, while many others would not, so when they chose the names for their children, each child's middle name had some kind of beneficial property about it. Your name, for example, Simon Tesla Templeton. Tesla was a scientist, but more than that, he was a genius of one. He knew how to use his mind to find the answers he sought. Everything he did, he made in the workshop of his mind first, quite literally. If it was a machine he wanted to build, for example, he built it in his mind first and he made certain it worked in his mind long before he ever built the real thing. Your sister's middle name is Prosperity, and look at her - she goes from strength to strength in everything she does. Why does this work? Because people live up to a name. It's the Laws of Thinking. You become what you think about."

"Names, surely not. Are you really saying that a person's name can be an influential factor in their life in terms of success?" Simon questioned sceptically.

"Yes, I am, and what is more, I am totally certain of the fact."

There was a slight pause as Ted and Simon pondered this. They both had smiles of speculation on their faces, combined with some humour. Almost as if a game of one-upmanship was about to start, where each player would take turns in outdoing their opponent in ever-increasing wild ideas and statements.

Simon started the next round by saying with a smile, "Do you think, or are you saying, that life's real losers should change their names in order to become more successful?"

Ted grinned, "Well, let me put it this way. What about all those times when you listen to the news on the radio, or watch it on TV, and you come across people and their name in some way or another matches their job title. Let me give you a handful of true real life examples that I have come across over the years. A policeman – PC Constable, a doctor called Dr Pain, a zookeeper by the name of Mr Wild, a farmer called Mr Bullock, a taxi driver by the name of Mr Miles. After the news, we get the weather report, and we find names like, Gale, Frost, Rainmore, and even Blizzard, I kid you not. I think the term for it is aptronym - A person's name, often regarded with some amusement in connection with their occupation."

Simon was just about to start his next round in the game when Ted excitedly cut back in, "No, no wait, here is my personal favourite, Sir William Lyons; he was one of the founders of Jaguar cars." At that, Ted began laughing, which led Simon to do the same. "Lyons – Jaguar, I ask you," said Ted, breaking down into even more laughter.

The game had now clearly fallen apart. It was not their best ever few rounds of the game of one-upmanship, but even so, it usually ended up in laughter. Still bubbling with laughter, Simon added, "What about that Jonny Cash?"

"And I'm sure he has plenty of it," Ted said with a new bout of laughter.

When they finally composed themselves again, Ted added, "All jokes aside, there truly is something in it, and there has been some serious research done on the topic, and a few books have been written on the subject, too. I think the real trick is in the good choice of a middle name. Your Mom and Dad were right about that one."

"We had better get back on topic, hadn't we Ted?" Simon suggested lightly.

"Yes, I agree, beware of distractions. Isn't that a life lesson, indeed?"

Ted stared into space for a moment, laying out his next thoughts. Then he took a deep breath in preparation, straightened himself up a little, and proudly began, "The thing that I really must tell you about the Laws of Thinking, the thing that you simply must know is …"

As Ted spoke these words, a light gust of wind blew across the table on this otherwise windless day. Simon noticed the breeze too, but the thing he noticed even more was how it had stopped Ted in his tracks. Ted's head remained still as his eyes slowly moved, almost with reluctance, in the direction of the telescope, almost like he was expecting something, so Simon focused on the telescope where Ted's eyes were fixed.

There was a second light gust of wind. The telescope turned 90 degrees on its tripod. Simon thought it odd that such a slight gust should even be able to move the telescope at all.

"Oh, blast," cried Ted, before his eyes moved back to Simon. Then he let out a heavy sigh, looking really disappointed, "We have much less time than I thought. That's your sign to go. I am sorry, but your time is up."

T-Junction to Change

Chapter 5

Simon was so surprised by Ted's abrupt change of course that he sounded a little put out when he replied, "I suppose you saw a vision of that moment, too?"

Ted gave a solemn nod in acknowledgement.

"Now wait a minute, Ted, I have missed my flight to travel here to see you at your request, and now you want me to leave when I have probably been here for less than an hour! I thought we'd make a day of it."

Ted looked blankly at Simon and raised his hands in an innocent gesture, "I am truly sorry, Simon, but you must be in the right place at the right time. I am only playing my part in the big scheme of things. We need to wrap this up now, this very moment, so you can get back in that lovely Jaguar XK8 of yours, and continue your adventure."

"What about the rest of it? You were just about to tell me something very important about the Laws of Thinking," Simon said with some insistence.

"Seek and you will find, Simon, seek and you will find. I have to let you go, right now," Ted uncharacteristically said in a panic after conversations that had seemed so casual and unhurried.

"What about this silly idea of you not being around tomorrow. Care to explain that?"

Ted said nothing further.

Simon stood up, as he resigned himself to the fact that this strange day had again given him yet another twist to deal with. He gestured to the microphone on the Dictaphone, wanting to end their time with a little humour, and said, "Any last quote from Ted today?"

Ted seemed to return to life momentarily, "Yes, why not, then you must go. In fact, I will give this quote to you and your soul mate to keep for your prosperity. Also may I say that I wish you both well and every success and happiness for the future. So, here it is, an Irish Blessing. 'May your troubles be less, and your blessings be more, and nothing but happiness come through your door.'"

At that, Ted pressed the stop button on the Dictaphone and handed Simon the box for it, so that Simon could take the Dictaphone with him throughout his future journeys, and perhaps listen to it from time to time.

Simon began packaging the Dictaphone. "Thank you, Ted, that was really nice." When he was finished, he asked curiously, "What are you going to do now, Ted?"

"There is so little time, and yet so much choice, just like life itself. One thing is for certain, I will stay here in the garden and enjoy the sunshine a while longer." Ted looked towards the assorted items on the table "I might drink a bit of that expensive red wine that I have been saving for a special occasion, but then, why go into the next world with your senses dulled by alcohol?

"After all, I have waited a lifetime to experience that tunnel of light thing; I would like to be fully aware as I travel up the tunnel of light into the next world. I could read a bit more of Almondie Shampine's fine book." But then he began gently tapping his headphones as he focused on the pile of music CD's and an entertaining thought entered his mind. "Maybe I should play my favourite Rachmaninoff CD, the one with his famous Piano Concerto No 2."

Ted chuckled with some real amusement at the idea of that. "That would be the trick. To finish this life in perfect timing with one of Rachmaninoff's big, classical, musical finishes." The thought amused him so much that he bellowed out in laughter, "But the trouble is, they would never cope at the other end with someone entering the next world all pumped by the emotional musical high of a Rachmaninoff big, classical finish."

Simon acknowledged him with a small smile, as he wasn't as amused at listening to his Granddad speak so casually of leaving this life.

When Ted had calmed back down again, he said, "I have also got my iPod in my pocket, too. Over a lifetime, I have collected so much great music, but how can you really choose what to listen to in those last few hours?" Ted finally settled his hand on *The Carpenter's* CD. "But for me, when it comes down to it, personally, I would choose the Carpenters. Boy can that Karen Carpenter ever sing, such amazing vocal tones, so skilfully and uniquely applied to each song - absolutely sublime. Across their many album tracks, there are so many little hidden gems. You have to get past that easy-listening term they got labelled with. To listen to Karen's heavenly voice one more time before I go, well, there is nothing wrong with that, is there."

For a moment, Ted became a little lost in thought. He looked reflective and gently nodded his head in appreciation of the CD.

Simon enquired, "Haven't you put that CD on your iPod too?" "I have indeed, I just prefer to handle the CD in its box and look through the booklet inside. In the past, those 12-inch records with the real big album covers were the best of all, but those days have gone now."

Ted removed his headphones from around his neck, then pulled the CD player from his belt and took his iPod from his trouser pocket. Then he sat back in his chair and cheerfully said, "There is plenty of time for music later on, but before any of that, it is time for a well-earned nap. I can sit here reflecting on a lifetime of memories, of a life well-lived, and drift off to sleep in the sunshine for a bit.

"And Simon, old boy, you had better be off now. As I've been saying, timing is very important to you and your new lady who is about to enter your life. A number of times in the coming hours you will both be in the same vicinity as each other, but it is very important that you do not meet at the wrong point in time. If you meet too early, or too late, you will both miss something very important to each of you. It is vital that you meet in exactly the right time, and exactly the right place."

Ted stood up to move his cast-iron antique-effect chair to face the sun more directly and then sat back down. When he was comfortably seated, he pressed a switch under the chair's right armrest, which then stirred a small electric motor into action. Simon watched, as first a footrest appeared from somewhere under Ted's chair and then the back rest of the chair extended to almost twice its original height, before reclining.

Ted winked at Simon and innocently asked, "What's up, it's my new toy," before slouching in his chair and sliding his golfing cap over his eyes to provide some shade.

"Good luck with your 360-degree tracked excavator, Ted. I am sure you will be fit and well when it arrives in a few days' time," Simon said, now more assured that Ted would be just fine, since he'd gone from talking about his final hours to saying he had plenty of time to first take a nap.

"Maybe I should give it to the village so that they can dig up some more of those stones," Ted said from under his hat.

"There's an idea."

There was a short pause from Ted, "Oh, when you meet her, tell her that Ted sends his regards."

"Goodbye for now, Ted." And with that, Simon walked back up the garden towards the house with his newly acquired Dictaphone in hand.

Reaching the corner of the house, Simon turned around to look back at Ted one last time, and thought to himself, *I am sure he will be all right.* Then he continued the short walk back to his Jaguar.

Despite the unusual events of the day, Simon had enjoyed his visit with Ted, as he had always done in the past. Simon was now feeling full of life and renewed energy again as he raced down the country lanes to the sounds of the Jaguar's wonderful engine.

Pulling up at a T-junction caused Simon to realise something very important, so he put the Jaguar's transmission into the park setting, and said aloud, "I don't know where I am going!" He shook his head, and chuckled at the new situation he now found himself in. "I haven't got a clue. So far, today has gone pretty much as directed by Ted. He even told me when I had to leave, but he never said where to?" Simon tried to pick apart anything in their conversations that may have provided a clue as to where Simon should go next.

Grandad had spoken of so many places and counties surrounding Wiltshire, all of which Simon remembered fondly from his childhood explorations with Ted the times he would visit. Grandad had loved taking him places and showing him the sites, before setting Simon up for a long-winded teaching moment that Simon had grown more and more to enjoy as he got older. But the sites, for certain, had always been spectacular.

This bit, and from here on, is obviously mine, Simon concluded. "The ball must be well and truly back in my court again now; well, that's something at least." He stared at the two destinations on the signpost of the T-junction. "I cannot sit here talking to myself all day. I will have to decide where I am going to go. If I turn right, and just drive, I imagine I will end up back at home. And if I turn left, and simply drive, I imagine I will end up in the city of Bath."

Still looking at the signpost, Simon thought to himself, *It is just like life - different choices will lead to different outcomes, but which is the right one?*

Simon needed just a little guidance to help make this important choice, so he put his right hand on his chest, near his heart, and looked right. Then, talking aloud again, he said, "Should I turn right?"

He paused for a moment before commenting, "Maybe, I am not going to be turning right today."

Then, without moving his hand from his chest, he looked left. "Should I turn left today?" He felt his heart beat rise at this suggestion. "Oh, confirmation. The city of Bath it is then."

He put the automatic transmission of the Jaguar back into drive before placing both of his hands back on the steering wheel and signalling left. "But, where should I go in Bath?

About 30 seconds went by before the answer came to him, "Oh yes, of course, and why not? I like that idea very much. Ted did say I have yet to complete step two in my turning point." Simon nodded to himself in agreement, and with a big grin on his face, too. "I am still on holiday anyway, am I not?"

He took his foot off the brake and pressed the accelerator pedal down as he said with anticipation, "Moonraker it is, then."

The Road to Bath

Chapter 6

Simon was back on the open road again and heading in the direction of Bath. He caught up with a lorry, which was driving slowly. On the back of the lorry was a brand new Massey Ferguson tractor.

As Simon followed the lorry, he took a closer look at the load it was carrying. He could see inside the cab of the new tractor, clear plastic-wrapping covered the new seat and the many controls and instruments inside the cab. The bright shining red paintwork on the body contrasted well with the silver and black artwork on the bonnet. Simon could appreciate that someone was going to get a fabulous boy's toy today and must be excitedly waiting for it to arrive.

This led him to thinking of Ted and their ending conversations. Surely, Ted would not have purchased a 30 tonne, 360-degree tracked excavator if he truly believed he would not be around to play with it. Besides, Simon had been having that vision with the hands and the ring for as long as he could remember, and it had yet to come to fruition, so Grandad may have seen his time ending, but that wasn't to say at all when it would actually occur.

He thought of his final conversations with Ted prior to leaving, one moment speaking of his time being very soon and the next of having all the time in the world.

Simon could not yet pass the lorry due to the amount of oncoming traffic. He checked his rear view mirror, only to see another bright red machine coming up fast behind him. As it drew closer, Simon easily recognised what it was, and looking at the number plate through his mirror, he could see that it too was brand new.

Directly behind Simon was another Jaguar, a red F-type convertible. Behind the wheel of the car was a girl with blonde long hair, which was flowing in the wind. The road ahead cleared, so Simon overtook the lorry, with the red F-type following him.

As Simon pulled back onto his side of the road, the red Jaguar continued picking up speed and held its position on the road to overtake Simon too. When they were both side by side, they briefly looked towards each other and smiled, but in no time at all, the red F-type was speeding up the road at nearly 100 mph.

Simon thought to himself, amused, *Two Jaguars racing up the road, and a blond in one of them. It's very tempting to play that game, but I don't think I will.*

As Simon continued driving, he was thinking about his imminent visit to Bath, and processing all that Ted had spoken to him about, and he decided that he couldn't turn up at the prestigious Moonraker Hotel with nothing but holiday T-shirts and shorts to wear, and with shoulder-length hair too. They would never let him in.

His life was experiencing a series of changes, all due to his turning point of a few days ago. Why not add to this series of changes before going to the Moonraker Hotel with a good haircut and some new clothes?

Simon realised that all gentlemen's barber shops would be fully booked on Saturdays, or at least they would have a long queue in them.

Simon thought it was time to manifest an empty barber shop, and a good car parking space, too. So Simon began to visualise an empty space at the front of the car park and an empty barber shop, as Ted had taught him when he was just a small boy. Obviously, he couldn't close his eyes while driving to visualise these two things, so instead, the visualisation took the form of mental expectation.

The journey did not seem to take too long, as Simon happily drove his Jaguar with the roof down in the bright sunshine of the day. Simon felt very much at home again when driving through the streets of Bath. All around him were the familiar sights of so much great architecture. Street after street of elegant, well-designed sandstone buildings, which made the City of Bath stand out as a city steeped in culture, history and heritage.

Simon was heading for the Charlotte Street car park, which bordered the truly beautiful Victoria Park, first opened in 1830 by the 11-year-old, Princess Victoria.

Simon was curious to see if his manifesting had worked. Would there be a good car parking space waiting there for him? On arrival at the front of the car park, he stopped to take a look. Every parking space, for as far as he could see, was full, but then, just at that very moment, the car closest to him backed out of its space and drove away. Simon said to himself "Perfect, just as I ordered," and drove right in.

Next, he rang the Moonraker Hotel from his mobile phone and booked a room for a few nights stay. Shortly thereafter, he was on foot and walking through the streets and heading to a barber shop he knew of. As he walked through the door of the barber shop, he passed the very last customer walking out.

Sitting in the barber's chair, as great lengths of his hair were being cut off, he thought to himself, *I manifested the perfect parking space, and an empty barber shop; it works every time. Yet, no one ever believes me when I tell them about it.*

"I have to admit, I love cutting off lots of hair when I get the chance," the gentleman barber made light conversation with Simon. "So many come in here for a light trim, but many of the older guys, especially, don't have too much to start with. Not too bad a job at it, either, if I don't say. You look like a whole new you," the barber turned Simon towards the mirror to admire his new haircut.

It was now much shorter and organized, elegant and refined, and a whole lot tidier. "A whole new me is exactly what I'm going for. Today is the day I change my stars and align myself with the Universe's plans for me," Simon commented happily.

"Ah, yes, makes perfect sense. You are on holiday and are looking to find your one," the barber winked at him while Simon looked on at him with surprise that he should know this.

"There are two types of people that frequent my shop. Those who want the same haircut that they've had for years, if not decades, and those looking for a change. It usually begins with a new haircut. Well, there is a third kind I need not mention," the barber chuckled, while rubbing at the bald spot atop his head. "It's either hats or a barber shop to perform a miracle for that third type."

"So, if those looking for change begin with a fresh hairstyle, then what do they look for next?" Simon said with amusement.

"Accessories," the barber gestured to Simon's wrist, "And a new wardrobe, which, dare I say, you are in desperate need of if you hope to complete your turning point. Very few can pull off your grandfather, Ted's, peculiar dressing habits."

"Peculiar, indeed, how -?"

"He stopped in a few days ago, told me you'd be here, and that I was to be a vital player in the course of your destiny. He had it in his mind that he would not have enough time to tell you everything, and you know, Ted, when he has something on his mind -"

"A whole new tree is sprouted," Simon chuckled.

Simon left the barber shop and spotted a wristwatch in the window of the jeweller's shop across the street. Even at this distance, it clearly stood out from the rest. It was gold in colour, chunky, yet elegant.

He glanced at the old, digital watch with a black plastic strap on his wrist that he'd had for ages and thought, *There is another change to make.*

As he walked across the street, he kept his eyes focused on the watch he had chosen, to be sure it was not something which only looked good at a distance, but if anything, the appearance of it kept improving as he drew closer. When he was standing directly in front of the window, he was certain it was the watch for him.

Simon turned to enter the shop door, and only then did he notice something in the next window, a window dedicated to displaying rings, and it stopped him in his tracks. "Oh my God ...Would you look at that?"

On the wall behind the trays of rings was a black and white promotional poster, and what it portrayed sent a shiver down his spine. The black and white poster showed a young woman's hand, with a man's hand sliding a wedding ring along the young lady's finger. The man's arm was also in the picture, in a dark jacket sleeve, with a white shirt and cufflink.

While the image was modern in appearance, it so much resembled the grey image Simon knew only too well from his recurring dream. For a brief moment, he felt weak, as if his energy was being drained right out of him.

When he noticed this happening, he made a positive effort to strengthen himself back up before asking himself, "Why is it, that since my turning point moment, these images have entered my mind more than ever, and now it appears that I even attract similar images to me?"

He entered the shop, already knowing what he wanted, what he'd been drawn to. The metal strap of the watch was adjusted to the right size for him, and the time correctly set. Without needless delay, he bought the watch. As he left the shop, feeling pleased with the new purchase now attached to his arm, he made a point of not looking at the poster in the window for a second time.

After all, now that he'd gotten the wheels spinning, positive momentum was pushing him towards what he wanted to achieve, so, without further ado, he made the short walk to Charringtons: Tailors of Distinction.

Like it had been at the jewellers, a quick glance through the front windows revealed the first thing he wanted to try on. He entered the shop wearing sandals, a t-shirt, baggy shorts, a refined haircut, and a very expensive watch.

There was an assistant standing near the till at the back of the shop, a middle-aged man, somewhat portly and rounded in stature, with a tape measure around his neck. As Simon walked across the shop towards the assistant, he noticed that the man never took his eyes off him, as though observing every detail of this potential customer. Up close the assistant appeared a little camp in his mannerisms, with slightly bulging eyes.

By the look on the assistant's face, Simon could easily imagine what the assistant was saying to himself in the privacy of his own mind, *Shorts and a t-shirt, how positively revolting.*

Simon raised both of his arms outstretched, like the statue of *Christ the Redeemer*, in *Rio de Janeiro* and said "Dress me well, please."

"It looks as if sir needs it," the assistant commented.

"I like the suit in the window."

"Of course, he said you would. An excellent choice, sir, shall I fetch the jacket for you to try on?"

"Please do." Simon disregarded the assistant's comment with bemusement, as, now that he thought of it, the Moonraker Hotel would normally be booked up at this time of year, yet Simon had had no problem at all getting a room. His Grandad had been busy indeed. *And what a waste it would have been, Ted, had I chosen to go on holiday with my friends, after all. Then what would you have done?* Simon thought. "Don't you need my measurements, first?" he said to the assistant.

"I noted down all your measurements the moment you walked in, sir. Years of practise."

A short time later, Simon had tried on the whole suit with matching shirt and tie, which became the first purchase sorted out. Returning from the changing room, wearing his pastime clothes, he found the assistant standing there waiting for him with an arm full of additional clothes. "Can I suggest something else for you, sir? Please come over to this full-length mirror, if you will."

"I suppose I can't make do with only one new change of clothes, now can I? Being in the right place at the right time only leaves me guessing where my journeys will lead me next and how long it might take," Simon commented.

"My thoughts exactly, sir," the assistant said while holding a well-tailored, brilliant, white silk shirt to Simon's chest and black trousers to his waist.

"You really do know your job well, I must say. If I had picked out a white shirt and black trousers, I would look like a waiter, but you would dress me in the same colours and make me stand out in the crowd," Simon said appreciatively.

"I am so glad sir approves, but please don't look at the price ticket or you will spoil the moment. Accessories, I am certain that sir would agree, a nice black belt with a chrome buckle, and shoes to match, would complete sir's transformation."

"Transformation, how did you guess?" Simon said with a slight grin, but the assistant did not reveal his source.

In less than an hour, Simon, with the very able help of the shop assistant, had chosen quite a number of items of clothing, all of which were more in line with his new image, and even more importantly, his new self-image, which was by far the most important thing.

He had just spent more money than he might have expected before he entered Charringtons, but he felt like a million dollars, his head held high, wearing his new white shirt and black trousers and all the matching accessories the skilful assistant had picked out for him.

Simon found himself rethinking the conversation with Ted regarding his first turning point in life, that Simon had thought was nothing but a complete fail, since his first self-owned business collapsed within a year. This failure or belief-of-failure had caused him to end up working beneath someone else, walking in their shadow, watching them win, and trying to accept his place in the world and settle, like everyone else, until he became fed up, hence, his turning point of only a few days ago.

Ted's perspective, on the other hand, had been focused on Simon's successes in that one year prior to the business's collapse, and the amount of money he had made, but now it was money well spent, which Simon hoped would bring him good fortune in the very near future.

When Simon returned to Charringtons in his Jaguar, much more fitting to his new look, in order to transport his many purchases to the hotel, the assistant's face was now much more appreciative and less prudish, since he found Simon to possess more refined taste, and most assuredly pleased with the profits made that day. Simon, himself, felt very satisfied with his time in Bath so far, even if he had done things a little bit more quickly than usual. Everything seemed to be happening so fast in just a few short days. He couldn't believe that it had only been this morning that he'd been heading out in one direction just to finish up where he was now, driving over the River Avon via Pulteney Bridge, which uniquely had shops on both sides of it, and then along Argyle Street to the roundabout at the end of it.

Simon took the first exit off the island, but not without glancing up Great Pulteney Street with all of its magnificent buildings, refinement and regal splendour, before turning left into the car park of the very prestigious Moonraker Hotel.

Directly in front of him was a bright red F-type Jaguar. He wondered if it was the same car belonging to the blonde lady racing past him earlier at 100 mph, tempting him with flirtatious play to race alongside her. The glance that he'd got of her had revealed that she was quite pretty and quite obviously a bit on the wild side. "Well, there is certainly nothing wrong with a free spirit, is there, especially one with good taste," he said aloud, while appreciating the sporty vehicle.

He looked around for a parking space. He wanted somewhere quiet to park his car, where it would not be getting knocked about by other car doors, or people shuffling past with bags and suitcases. He looked for the area of the car park farthest away from the hotel doors where people were less likely to park and do that old-fashioned thing called walking in today's fast-paced world. Simon, on the other hand, enjoyed fast cars, sure, but more than that, he liked time to look about the world and appreciate it. Apparently, he wasn't the only one.

"What on Earth is that?" Simon said in total wonder after catching sight of the only other vehicle parked in the quiet area of the car park, furthest from the hotel. He drove across the car park and parked two spaces down from the vehicle which had caught his attention. "Wow, and how amazing is that? Who in the world would drive something like that? I am in total admiration of them."

He got out of his car to take a closer look at the vehicle. Simon thought it funny how talking with Ted earlier today a Toyota Land Cruiser had come up in the conversation, as that was exactly what he was looking at now, but there couldn't be another Toyota Land Cruiser like this one, anywhere.

This Toyota Land Cruiser appeared to be an ex-safari park vehicle, and it was all painted up in tiger colours. Golden orange and black stripes with the words 'Safari Park' in big letters on all four sides, but to add to the curiosity of this vehicle, the name of the Safari Park it had previously belonged to had been roughly brush-painted over, making this already distinctive vehicle stand out even more.

This four-wheel drive was also a bit of a classic vehicle too, a 1982 Toyota Land Cruiser, model J60 station wagon, big and chunky in appearance, customized further with four wide-rimmed, very shiny, classic chrome, Wolfrace wheels.

Most ex-safari park vehicles of any type usually had very hard lives and were full of big dents, but this Toyota Land Cruiser, despite its age, was in absolutely mint condition. Simon took a quick look inside at the interior, which was in great condition. All in all, he thought the vehicle was absolutely amazing, but who would drive such a thing and why?

Simon came away from his reverie at the sound of small wheels, one with a bit of a squeak, growing louder behind him. He turned around to see one of the hotel porters heading towards him with a suitcase trolley. The porter, noticing Simon's interest in the Toyota, said, "It probably belongs to a Hen party or group of guys on a Stag weekend. You would be amazed what some of them turn up in."

Simon walked over to the boot of his car to open it. He observed the porter looking appreciatively at his own vehicle and fixing his eyes on Simon's new watch as it caught the sunlight. He then turned his attention to the contents of the boot. "Someone has been to Charringtons, I see. That is a very expensive shop, but one of the finest tailors in England. Many of the people who stay in this hotel pay a visit to Charringtons while they are here, and all of them speak well of it," the porter commented while loading Simon's various items onto his trolley.

"If you don't mind me saying so, looking at your luggage, you appear to be someone who has come to Bath at short notice."

"You are indeed correct about that," Simon acknowledged as they both began walking towards the hotel's entrance. "This is my first visit to the Moonraker Hotel. It has been on my to-do list for a long time."

The sociable porter continued to make conversation. "Well here you are, and this hotel is now seven years old as of last weekend. A purpose-built hotel and conference centre. As a hotel, it is one of the largest and finest in the City of Bath, with all the usual refinements: a gym and fitness centre, a sauna, swimming pool, and a top-class restaurant. We have large gardens at the rear which overlook the River Avon. There are three conference rooms, and the biggest of them can hold around a thousand people. Best of all, this totally modern building has been built to truly fit in with the surrounding area, hence the elegant use of sandstone in its external design. Are you here for a conference this weekend? Our main conference room is holding an event all weekend for the British Oratory Excellence Organisation. You know, public speaking and all that kind of thing. It is their big speech contest weekend, I believe."

"No, I am here on holiday … I think? Well, I hope so anyway, but I feel anything could happen after the day I have had."

The chatty porter had succeeded in gaining Simon's interest and he was really looking forward to viewing the inside of the hotel for the first time, but once they made their way through the revolving doors, it was like nothing he had been expecting. The whole place looked like a building site. Whatever had stood in the centre of the lobby had been removed. Builders were busy erecting a large wooden wall while other construction workers used jackhammers to dig up the floor.

Simon turned to the porter and enquired above the noise, "What is going on here?"

"Well, that is a good question, and one I do not have the full actual answer to. It is all a very big secret. The only thing management will tell any of us is they're going to put something in the centre of the lobby that is a world-first. Whatever it is, they say that no other hotel in the world has one. More than that, I can't say, but it sounds like something pretty amazing and well worth seeing once it's complete."

As they waited for the receptionist to finish a phone call, one hand plugging the ear that she didn't have the phone to, in order to hear the caller above the noise, Simon looked around him. The lobby had quite a number of people in it, spilling out from the corridor which led to the conference rooms. Mostly, they were standing around in groups and talking, all of them wearing a delegate badge for the British Oratory Excellence Organisation annual speech contest the porter had spoken of.

"Hello again, Mr Green Jaguar man," a friendly-sounding voice said beside him. "Nice haircut too."

Simon instantly recognized her as the attractive blonde who owned the red F-type Jaguar. Before he could say a word, she continued walking past him to rejoin her group of friends. Simon did not fail to notice that her eyes swept over him from his head to his shoes and back up again and the appreciation he saw in them when she met back up with his eyes, just before they all walked back towards the conference rooms.

So she liked to play cat and mouse, did she? Simon grinned. He considered upping the ante a bit and baiting her in the same way she appeared to be baiting him, by showing her a bit of his own free spirit. However, he recalled Ted's words about the significance of it being exactly the right place at exactly the right time or important things would go missing from the whole experience, so he was determined to say nothing and let her walk away. All the while patiently awaiting the next course of events, and perhaps, and hopefully, in Simon's mind, their next random meeting, wherever and whenever it might be.

Night in Bath

Chapter 7

Simon settled into his room three floors up. It was a spacious room with all the amenities and conveniences the porter had promised, he even took the time to assist Simon in his unpacking, for which he received a very gracious tip in exchange. All of Simon's new clothes were now either hung up or folded in a drawer. He felt more at home in this elegant hotel room than he had for years in his apartment back in his own home city.

His window did not overlook the River Avon, rather provided a view of the main car park, which he preferred, anyway, as he looked out at the mysterious blonde's red Jaguar, and even more mysteriously, the tiger-striped Toyota Land Cruiser still parked in the far corner, amusingly seeming to be guarding his own green Jaguar.

He moved to the mirror to look over himself, he somehow simultaneously looked exactly as he should look without looking like himself at all.

"Most people don't take a second look in the mirror. They don't question their lives or think about where they're going or what they're doing, yet they're the cry-babies in the world saying it's all unfair." Ted had said during their earlier conversation.

After Simon had failed at his one business endeavour, he had become the guy with hair that never saw a barber, content with the ease and affordability of baggy shorts and t-shirts and a go-nowhere job. He'd rented the first flat he looked at, not bothering to look elsewhere, and stayed with the one girl he'd dated, while not looking elsewhere, all while not even considering their commitment, or any progressive movement forward whatsoever. He'd just believed himself content with what he had while actively ignoring any wayward thoughts that said otherwise, up until the point that she had provided him with the ultimatum of having to think of such things, thereby allowing her to walk out the door without trying to stop her.

She had forced him to look at things. She had forced him to think. And those thoughts had led him to the realisation that he no longer wanted to be that guy. So, in effect, she had lost him, not the other way around. He wondered what she would think of him now.

"This is quite a transformation from the boy I thought I was, but this is who I am, and it's just the beginning," he said aloud in approval of the reflection looking back at him.

Then he sat on the bed and turned on his small laptop, in readiness to upload the contents of his new Dictaphone. There were various cables that Ted himself had had difficulty with, trying to find out which went where, so he opened the instruction manual on the contents page and very briefly looked over the chapter titles. Already bored, he said, "That is enough time spent reading the instructions."

And with that, he threw the instruction manual on the bed.

After spending, perhaps too much time with the trial-and-error method of fitting this into that and declaring what happens ifs and thens, he finally successfully uploaded the digital audio files from the Dictaphone to his laptop, added them to his iTunes app, and copied them on to his Cloud account in order to have the audio safely stored away in more than one location to take care of the just-in-cases as well.

"I really have paid a high price for that audio, in time and a lost holiday, so I will be sure to get the most of it, by listening to it from time to time. There really must be some reason, in the big scheme of things, to all the events of today." He looked at his new watch, which told him that it was now 5:30pm.

"And I have missed lunch too! What a day. I should not think too deeply into the events of the day and what has already happened. Rather, I should be thinking about the present moment and what I'm to do next, which, to my thinking, is to get an evening meal and chill-out a bit. I've earned that much. Besides, I doubt I'll be meeting my eternal soul mate in the comforts and confines of my room."

Which was only confirmed when he found that both the red Jaguar and tiger-striped Toyota Land Cruiser had left since he last looked out his hotel window.

After leaving the Moonraker Hotel, he walked over Pulteney Bridge and was very soon in the heart of Bath. He made his way to Old Bond Street and then on to New Bond Street, where there were a good amount of choices for places to eat and drink.

Simon felt very at ease and natural walking through the streets of Bath amongst people of all nationalities. He had always felt this city had a genuine multicultural feel about it, and it had always felt like a safe and friendly city to be in. Some cities made the claim of being multicultural, yet they were more based on tolerance than true harmony, causing a visitor to feel uncomfortable and not quite welcome. In a real multicultural city, harmony could be seen in the smiles on peoples' faces, and felt by the relaxation and ease of those in one another's company.

Simon spotted a public house with tables and chairs outside, which quite nicely matched his visualisation of the ideal place to sit down, have some food and drink, and watch the world go by.

In a doorway, only a very short distance away from the pub's outside tables and chairs, sat a young man staring at the floor. He looked down on his luck, a cap lying open on the ground before him for people passing by to drop some unwanted pocket change into.

Simon found just that in his pocket and dropped it into the man's cap, which was followed by an Australian male voice bellowing out, "What you do that for? He will only buy alcohol with it."

Simon looked in the direction of the voice and saw a large man sitting at one of the pub's tables, while holding on to a full pint of beer in his hand. The irony of what he had just said while drinking himself was not lost on Simon, who returned the man's comments with, "As the old saying goes: 'There but for the grace of God go I.'"

The young man in the doorway quietly said thank you while continuing to stare at the floor, looking all worn and torn as though the world had beaten him.

Simon entered the pub and walked up to the bar when he heard someone behind him say, "Well, well, if it isn't my old mate Simon."

The barman entered his side of the bar and came into view and Simon instantly recognized him. "Oh, hello Mick, how are you doing? Fancy seeing you here. I thought you went off to the USA. Florida, wasn't it?"

"Fancy, is seeing your new look. I almost didn't recognize you. Florida is where I went all right, but things did not turn out for me over there like I had planned, so I thought I would give Bath a try."

"Well it is good to see you again, Mick, though I might add that I believe I saw you wearing the same exact thing last time I saw you." Nor was the irony lost on Simon, his friends' both welcoming and parting words in regards to Simon's own attire earlier. It was impossible to believe that all these changes had occurred in just one day, made more profound in seeing that Mick looked exactly the same.

"I tell you what Simon, I have got just the pint for you to try. It is one of our new guest beers and it only came in yesterday. How do you fancy a pint of Amnesia? It is very good, but for some reason, after pouring it, it takes ages to clear, I do believe, but you forget about the wait after you've had the one. Having to wait for the second is probably a good thing."

"With a name like Amnesia, it sounds just the right thing for me today. You know what they say. Out with the old. In with the new, which is exactly in line with what I am trying to achieve today. Pour one for me, will you, Mick?"

Simon picked up a bar-food menu from the rack on the side of the bar while Mick slowly poured Simon a pint of Amnesia.

"So what have you been up to today, Simon, what brings you here?"

"I spent some time with Ted today."

"Oh, he is a great guy, old Ted. Knows a few things too. I have always got time for him. Actually, now that I think of it, I saw

Ted the other day. He was driving that Ford Mustang of his through Bath, zipping along so fast, he didn't even see me waving at him. I saw him again later on, walking down the street. You would never guess what he was wearing?"

Simon laughed a little before saying, "Please don't tell me."

"There you are, old friend, one pint of Amnesia. As you can see, it is a bit cloudy, but it will clear … eventually."

"Thanks, Mick, great seeing you again, but I think I'll take a seat outside while the weather is permitting and decide upon what I would like to eat on this very unusual day. Bye for now."

Simon chose a table, his back facing the wall. The beer-drinking Australian sat nearby, facing him. He looked at his pint of Amnesia, which was cloudy and seemed ages away from clearing, and thought, *Mick, he is a right one, all right. I will never forget the time he blew-up the science lab at our school. I bet this pint never clears.*

Simon took a closer look at it. First, he looked at it from directly above it. Then, he lowered his head to the height of the table and stared directly into it, watching the swirling liquid inside the glass as it slowly sorted itself out.

The Australian coughed, as if to point out that he was watching Simon. "Have you lost your fish, mate?" the Australian loudly enquired.

Well, two can play at this game, Simon thought to himself, so he put on an exaggerated, high-class English accent, and replied, "Don't worry, old boy, he cannot hide from me for too much longer."

Trying to avoid the direct line of sight between him and the Australian, Simon moved his head around to the right and looked into the side of the glass.

"Blimey mate, are you going to drink that thing or what?"

Before Simon could think of a suitable reply, a young female Japanese voice said, "Excuse … hello."

Simon slowly sat upright again in his chair to find an attractive-looking Japanese girl, around about 19 to 20 years old, smiling in amusement at seeing him looking into the side of his drink.

"You English, very funny peoples."

She had two other very attractive-looking Japanese friends, also around 20 years old, standing almost directly behind her.

Simon thought to himself, One, two, and three - is this something Ted should have told me about? They all very much resembled one another in hair, height, and stature, but their demeanour seemed quite a bit different, with number one obviously being the speaker of the group.

"Do you know … Where are horses?"

"Horses?" Simon asked in puzzlement, and then added, "Your broken English is much better than my non-existent Japanese. Sorry, but I do not understand … horses?"

The girl in front smiled and nodded enthusiastically. Number two, the girl in the middle, had a concerned look on her face. Number three at the back just giggled nervously.

"Horses … urm … oh, white horse … yes, white horses."

Simon looked over in the direction of the Australian for a lead, but the large man just sat there with a smirk on his face, completely at ease with being amused at Simon's expense.

"This is Bath, there are no horses here. Perhaps you mean white house?"

She insistently replied, "White horses."

"Blimey mate, it's about as clear as your pint." The Australian laughed aloud for the entire world to hear.

Simon inspected his pint, which hadn't got any closer to clearing, then returned his attention to the girls, where number one hadn't lost her conviction at all that Simon could help them. Number two looked even more worried, and number three giggled even more upon eye contact. The pretty girl in the middle whispered rapidly in Japanese to the first girl, whom then looked like she remembered something, so firmly and almost defiantly said, "Chalk."

Then she smiled with renewed confidence at Simon, as if that one word cleared up everything, while Simon looked her in the eye, having no idea at all what she might mean.

Simon thought he had better reiterate the little information he had, in the vain hope of finding some meaning, "Chalk, white horses; in Bath." He held out his hands, as though he was holding the reins of a horse. All three enthusiastically smiled while nodding in agreement.

For Simon, it had been a long day, a day which had already had its fair share of odd moments. Maybe it was obvious, but horses in Bath?

Finally, the Australian came to Simon's rescue. "You Pommy; honestly, you don't even know your own bloody country, mate." The Australian made a great show of standing up, pulling a leaflet out of his pocket, and smacking it down on Simon's table before returning to his seat.

"Ah." Simon sighed in grateful realisation, "I understand now. White horses are not in Bath. They are scattered around the countryside. On chalk hills, in fact."

He showed the leaflet to the excitable girl in front and pointed at the relevant areas. "You will have to take a coach trip to see them. Look, there is a map on the back of the leaflet."

"Oh, thank me," the first one said happily and spoke in Japanese to her friends, whom all nodded understanding. Then the worried girl in the middle whispered something to the girl in front. She looked upward to the left, racking her memory for the correct English word, and then said, "Self me."

The Australian belted out another loud laugh to see Simon struggling again.

"Self me?" Simon enquired in returned confusion.

"Self me," Number one repeated, like it should be obvious. Then number two produced a camera.

Simon felt relief, once again, "Oh I see, 'Self me'. Should be selfie, but actually, you mean photo."

He took the camera as they joined together for a group photo. Simon thought he would try some silent humour to cut through the awkward language barrier a little, so he pretended to take a photo of himself, saying, "Selfie", aloud as he did so.

The girl in the middle looked on at him in shock, while the third one continued giggling and the first one insisted, "Self Me. Self Me," while gesturing towards the three of them.

"Gotcha," Simon said light-heartedly, smiling in good fun.

The Australian looked on bemused, while Simon, trying to look cool, turned the camera around 180 degrees in his hand to face them, but then dropped it on the table, nearly knocking over his pint.

"Blimey Pommy … Strewth," the Australian hollered in laughter.

Simon apologetically picked up the camera again and pointed it at the group. He was just about to tell them to smile when the Australian said, "Smile and say cheese."

"Cheese?" the first girl questioned in confusion, but then they all smiled at Simon while he took the picture. Only then did Simon notice that the screen of the camera was now on self-portrait. When he had dropped it, it must have changed the setting, so now the picture Simon had just taken was actually of him, and not the group of three.

Before Simon had a chance to point this out, number one whisked the camera out of his hands, followed by multiple thank yous from the three of them and their quick departure thereafter.

Simon turned to the Australian and thanked him for his help in producing the leaflet. "Though it was right in front of my face, I do believe I would not have figured it out without you."

"No problem, mate. It's what I am here for."

Simon finally had a moment to look over the menu where he decided on the pie & chip dish with a side salad. He went inside to order the meal, but when he returned, he noticed the Australian's seat was now empty and there appeared to be no sign of him.

Simon looked at his pint, which was still a bit cloudy. He shook his head and asked himself, "What was all that about? Such an odd day, indeed." Simon's thoughts returned again to the events of the day, mostly the conversations with Ted and those instances where Ted had seemed to want so urgently share his knowledge with Simon, especially regarding *her*, whom Ted claimed to be his eternal soul mate, but it was like Ted had said in regards to the information being too much and the human mind not being able to hold it all, Ted kept branching off into a multitude of different subject matters, while not being able to thoroughly explain a single one, because there were just too many.

Clearly, some deep thinking would be needed before long, to help Simon fit all the many pieces together in order to make further progress in completing his turning point, especially that point of giving to the Universe. What would he give and how would he give it in order to receive?

He also gave some thought to his reaction when he had seen that poster in the jewellers shop window this afternoon, and how much it had affected him.

"Oh, how that damn dream of mine haunts me, even more so these past few days, but what does it all mean?"

Simon looked into the crowd of faces all around him and pondered on his true soul mate. Was she somewhere out there now, amongst the thousands of people in Bath? Could she be the attractive blonde with the red sports car? Perhaps one of the members of the British Oratory Excellence Organisation? She could walk into the pub at any moment now, providing a good reason as to why he was still sitting here, not a sip of alcohol in his system, while waiting for his damn drink to clear.

Maybe she too was out there looking for him? The two images from the recurring dream of his entered his mind yet again, even more vividly than before as he made the connection that the ring being removed from the lifeless hand was the same ring in the second scene being buried. Then he began seeing something that he'd never noticed before, as he'd always been so focused on watching the hands digging fastly at the wet soil, something so familiar, almost as though he knew the place, like he'd been there before. And not just once. Many, many times before, but what was this place? Where was it?

He paced his breathing, looking further and further within, in an effort to meditate as Ted's words now made complete sense, "Seek and You Will Find". He needed to find the answers that his subconscious was trying to provide to him by producing the recurring images to begin with.

But then suddenly, the loud Australian voice woke Simon abruptly out of his deeply relaxing state, "There you go, my Pommy mate," and two pints of beer landed with a thud on the table by the side of Simon's cloudy pint. "Why don't you drink this one instead? That thing of yours will never clear. I think you have earnt it after all the entertainment you have given me. Life is too short to wait for a good beer. Between you and me, I think the barman is a right wanka."

Simon made an attempt at thanking the burly man, but the boisterous Australian took no time to pause as he picked up Simon's pint of Amnesia, "Tell you what Pom, let me follow your act of kindness. I think you are right, I am sure our mate in the doorway over there would like a drink too, wouldn't he? This one will do, since you've done nothing but look at it wondering why you got it in the first place."

Simon finally enjoyed his first taste of a refreshing, cold beer, his food forgotten about at the moment – seems the Amnesia had done its job after all – as the Australian very loudly decreed, "This is for you, mate," to the young man in the doorway.

The boy's eyes brightened and appeared much more alive, and he held it up as a toast to the two men, before returning his focus and wasting no time at all in taking a hardy sip of the potent beverage, while trying very hard not to down it in one. One simple act of kindness and he had gone from looking very beaten down and scared of the world to taking on the appearance of being truly happy.

"It looks as if he is going to enjoy that," Simon commented. The Australian and Simon raised their own beers and tapped them together, both shouting "Cheers" in unison, with Simon purposely trying to be louder than the loud man. Since the Australian had chosen just that moment to not attract the attention of the world, Simon once again fell privy to his new friend's amusement on his behalf.

"I am Simon, what might your name be?"

"Charles. I don't know what my Dad was thinking of when he gave me a name like that! Do I look like a bloody Charles to you?"

"Can't say as you do. I think Titan would be much more fitting, don't you think?" This time they both fell into fits of laughter.

Over the next two hours, the two men laughed and joked about all kinds of unrelated subjects. Simon had his pie & chips and they both drank pint after pint of the good stuff.

Journey to the Subconscious

Chapter 8

It was still early evening as Simon headed back to the Moonraker Hotel; now feeling the most relaxed he had all day, due to a few laughs and plenty of beer. He decided to take the long way around to get back to his hotel, thinking that a good long walk, with a few gentle hills along the way, would be good exercise and would help to sober him up a bit.

At first, he staggered a little, like someone who had drunk a bit too much, but after some time, he found a good walking pace and was able to take in all the many sites and scenery that Bath had to offer.

Many times in the past, Simon had walked amongst the streets of Bath and admired the fine stone buildings of this World Heritage City. He believed it could take a lifetime to explore a city like Bath as the more you looked, the more you found. There was so much rich, hidden detail to be explored, everywhere you looked, and an equal amount of history too.

After some time, Simon found himself on the Cleveland Bridge, which was once a toll bridge for the city of Bath, a great many years ago. The distinctive bridge still retained the look of a toll bridge, but now it was a grade 2 listed building. Simon stopped halfway across the bridge and looked down upon the flowing River Avon. Mature trees with their green leaves that stood along each river bank added a beautiful contrast to the stone buildings nearby.

It was a nice spot to stand on a warm summer's evening. His mind began to wander as he reflected on some of his many happy visits to Bath over the years. Then, out of the blue, the first image from his recurring dream played forth visually in his mind, closely followed by the second image, slightly annoying him for having disturbed his moment of tranquil enjoyment by the river.

"I must do something about this, but what?" Simon turned away from the river and stared at the pavement for a moment as he contemplated what must be done to stop this. He now began purposely walking again towards the Moonraker Hotel, his mind becoming increasingly troubled as he focused his thoughts on only one thing - finding some answers.

"The first time the image came to me when I was awake, instead of its usual form in my dreams, was the moment I looked at Mona's hand when she spoke of marriage," he began backtracking events and experiences in his mind, like one retracing their steps in order to find something they had lost.

"Then there was the period of time after she left, the moments I was kicking myself in the behind for letting her go, when the images would replay themselves. Then they began to follow me wherever I would go, disrupting all my normal goings-on, so that at home, at work, out with my usual associates and friends, I couldn't be free of them, because as disturbing as they are, they pull me in a way, in a sense, into something I can't explain, in a way I've never felt before. Everything else seemed so inconsequential in comparison."

"That's when I first looked in the hypothetical mirror and decided I wasn't happy and I was fed up and I wanted change.

Only then did I have the dream of the Jaguar, my Jaguar, that appeared right across the street, just as I'd seen it in my dream, and then I bought it, just as my dream had foretold."

Simon was so deep in thought that when he crossed the hotel car park, he didn't notice any of the cars in it, which had caught his imagination before. He entered the lift and rose to the floor of his room. Walking down the corridor, his mind felt sharp and clear - the long walk and exercise having helped to wear off the beers. "Having splurged on such an impulsive purchase for the first time, and finally beginning to feel the change within myself, I then took it to the next level, told my boss I was taking leave on all my unused holidays and scheduled the ten-day holiday with my friends. That night, I dreamed of the airport, seeing my friends across the room at the departure gates, walking to join them, and then the phone call that would then disrupt all my plans."

"On Ted's insistence, and curiosity alone, since my dreams had awarded me with my Jaguar, I cancelled my plans and instantly headed out to Grandad's, where at times he seemed to be talking nonsense up until the point where he knew all these things that he shouldn't have. Now, here I am, in a place I am glad I am at, but had no intention of being. I've cut my hair. I've a new watch, and I spent what I make in a year on an entirely new wardrobe and a prestigious hotel, all on a whim. Yet now, the images are harassing me more than they ever have before."

Simon distractedly removed his shoes and sat upon his bed, completely focused on his thoughts. "I can't possibly keep up at this pace. Things are just happening so quickly, so fast, yet I'm hardly being allowed time to enjoy myself and enjoy the scenery, and take things one moment at a time, due to these blasted images."

Simon recalled his Grandad telling him he was on the Universe's timetable now, not his own, and that confusion was a healthy effect of it all. Being as how it's the Universe and eternity, you would think it'd be at a much slower pace than things with time limitations, such as humans, but then it made sense. Simon was running out of time to fulfil the Universe's plans for him, as he'd wasted far too much time maintaining a path he wasn't supposed to have been on, or at least, one he wasn't meant to stay on for as long as he had.

He now fully realised that time was of the essence, so he continued deep in thought. "There must be a lot more to these dreams. If they have any real meaning and value at all, then they will only be fragments of something bigger, like the images I keep seeing that are only fragments of something I'm trying to understand," he said quietly to himself.

Then in a tone of challenge, he said both aloud and forcefully, "Okay, recurring dreams, you must tell me more or else be still and leave me alone."

Simon was still not sure what to do, but he thought something was about to unfold. His eyes wandered around the room, as if searching for a clue. They landed on a pile of magazines and the room service menu, which sat on a chair in the corner.

He rubbed his forehead with both hands while he continued to stare at these particular items that had caught his attention. Then his mind wandered a bit to the attractive Japanese girls that had interrupted him when he was just about to look at the menu to order food. 'Self me', and his Australian friend saying, 'Smile and say cheese,' he recalled with a chuckle. Slowly, a smile appeared on his face, as he realised the answers he sought might now be very close at hand.

The sound of his hands dropping from his forehead and landing on his lap preceded the deep breath he drew, the raising of his head so his chin was pointed up, as he confidently said, "Cheese." Nodding his head in acknowledgment, Simon now knew he had found the answer that he was looking for, so he began pacing the floors excitedly.

"Cheese, oh yes, cheese. Why didn't I realise this before? I try always to avoid the stuff, but such things can't always be avoided when I so like cheese. The very first night I had that dream of the ring and the hand, I was but a child. I remember it so well now. How I admired the delicate hand with the ring, as it reminded me of my Mom's, and though the image of the male's hand was of a grown-ups, I knew it was mine, but then I felt the ice of her fingers, how cold they were, and how they did not move as mine did, and that's when I awoke horrified, because I realised the hand belonged to someone who was dead.

"It was New Year's Eve that night. My parents had thrown a splendid party. At least, that's what they called it. I just remember the food, so much food, but mostly the rich, flavoured cheese that I couldn't eat enough of. Then I had that dream, so ever since, it has been just one of those things unique to me. Cheese equals bad dreams, or something of that sort.

Simon picked up the room service menu and thumbed through it until he came to the cheese board selection. There were three variations of cheese board to choose from, and Simon was in his glory. Simon so loved cheese, yet he'd deprived himself of it for ages. "Don't you just love this hotel," he said in refined English. "One could get used to this very quickly."

Now certain of how he was going to find his answers, he picked up the phone for room service. "Hello, Simon Templeton here, in room 337. Could you send up the Wessex cheese board selection to my room, please?"

"Would you like anything else, sir?" Enquired the voice on the end of the phone, "A red wine perhaps?"

"You are right, of course. You can't eat cheese and biscuits without something to wash it down with." Hurriedly, Simon picked up the wine list, "A Merlot, perhaps. That goes well with most things."

"It does indeed, sir. We have several brands of Merlot to offer, but might I suggest our top-shelf brand that you cannot find in any -"

"Yes, yes, that sounds fine. Oh, and a couple of bottles of still water, too." Simon interrupted, not wanting to waste any further time when he was so close to finding what had eluded him for so long. He was feeling energised again and full of purpose.

He quickly undressed himself and walked into the bathroom. He had a quick shave, followed by a quick shower, before putting on a Moonraker bath robe that was so luxurious and accommodating, yet natural, that Simon had another moment of the simultaneous feeling of being exactly where he belonged, while feeling out of place at the same time. He figured it was the transition between letting go of his prior life and embracing one that better suited him. His turning point evolving into his new life, when they say that change is difficult due to such out-of-place feelings, even if things feel more right than they did before.

There was a knock at the door before room service entered, carting his Wessex cheese board selection, and, he was sure, a very expensive bottle of Merlot, and two bottles of water. He tipped handsomely, as money had no means at the moment, and then went on to look at the impressive selection of cheese and biscuits on the tray.

Feeling quite like the child who had engorged himself on cheese that night long ago when he had first had that dream, he said to himself, "This should do the trick."

He poured himself a glass of red wine and lifted it up to his nose, taking in the aromas of the wine before taking a sip to sample it. His prior self had only gone with the cheapest of wines, the ones in pretty bottles that his girlfriend, then, seemed to take a liking to on every anniversary and occasion she could think of. Nearing the end of their breaking point, he'd been bringing a bottle home to her every night.

He'd never much fancied the stuff, but now, he kept the liquid on his tongue, moving it in little waves in his mouth while savouring all the many different flavours that seemed to entice all of his varying taste buds, the sweet, the sour, the bitter, and so much more.

As though he'd been exploring wines his entire life, he said, "A very good choice, if I may say so myself. They stock a good wine cellar here, too. Strictly speaking, you should not really mix the grape and the grain, or so the saying goes. According to Mick, the saying in America is that beer before liquor makes you sicker, so I'm sure it follows suit with wine as well, but these are unusual times for me, and if the cheese and combination of beer and wine doesn't get me dreaming, then there is always the minibar later on to stir things up a little more."

Simon set himself up on the bed to relax and enjoy what remained of the evening, with his wine on the side table to his right and the tray of food to his left on the bed. With the TV remote in hand, he searched for an enjoyable film to watch. The best part of an hour and a half went by eating cheese with crackers and drinking red wine while an old film played in the background before finally tiredness caught up with him. He got off the bed, placed his food tray on the side table, dropped off his robe and crawled sleepily into bed. Not too long after turning off the table lamp and placing his head on the pillow he was fast asleep.

0-0-0-0

An unknown amount of time went by before a series of dreams started, beginning with random and seemingly meaningless scenes and images from his day. In the first dream, he saw himself sitting on the pavement with a cap placed directly in front of him. The cap had some coins already in it, and as he looked at the coins, three more coins were thrown into the cap from above. He looked up to see the blonde lady, Miss Red Jaguar, leaning over the top of her car door throwing in even more coins.

Still sitting, he looked over to his right to see Charles, his Australian beer-drinking friend, sitting at a table with the young beggar man from earlier that day, both of them laughing and joking as they drank beer together. The young beggar, who had been down on his luck before, was now dressed in all Simon's fine clothes from Charringtons – Tailors of Distinction.

Dreams continued to skip from scene to scene, without the need for perfect continuity. Simon saw himself standing in front of the table, where the two men sat, and asking them, without receiving any reply, "Where's my beer?"

To his left, he heard a seductive female voice say, "I've got something better than beer." The two men vanished from the scene of the dream, and the blonde lady, the driver of the Jaguar, now stood directly in front of him. She resembled Uma Thurman as seen on the movie posters for the movie Kill Bill, where Uma Thurman was portrayed wearing a bright yellow jumpsuit with a long zipper down the front of it. However, the lady standing in front of him now was wearing a bright red jumpsuit to match her Jaguar.

She lifted up her right hand, took hold of the zip pull-tab, and slowly started to pull down the zipper, revealing more and more well-rounded and well-tanned cleavage as the zip travelled lower. As she did this, she said in an even more seductive tone than before, "Why don't you spend some quality time with me?"

An unknown amount of time passed before the second dream started, with an even greater collage of ill-fitting images than the first. It began with Simon walking around the corner of Ted's house, to find Ted dressed like a circus ringmaster with a red coloured, long-tailed ringmaster's jacket, a tall black hat, and a long black cane. This image of Ted clearly represented the part he had played as the master of ceremonies and events of the previous day.

Simon noticed that Ted's garden was a real mess. No longer did it have manicured lawns, rather mounds of soil were dug up everywhere. Ted tapped his black ringmasters cane against the 360-degree tracked excavator, which didn't appear until he tapped it. There, in the middle of the garden, stood this enormous bright orange machine.

"Simon, my boy, why don't you take her for a spin?" Ted said.

"What shall I dig?"

"Why dig the cheese, Simon, dig the cheese."

Without asking anything further from Ted, Simon walked over to climb aboard the excavator. Only then did he notice something about it had changed.

"Where have the tracks gone, Ted? Where have the tracks gone?"

The top half of the excavator, the part which rotated, was no longer on tracks. Instead, it sat atop Ted's Ford Mustang Mach 1.

"Don't worry Simon, my boy, it's a *Ford*, it'll take it." Ted reassured.

Simon then found himself at the controls of the excavator, but instead of the usual two control levers coming up from the floor, the only method of control was the steering wheel of Simon's green Jaguar convertible with its chrome leaping Jaguar emblem.

Simon looked to his right through the doorway of the excavator just as Ted pulled up alongside him, driving the tiger-striped Toyota Land Cruiser. Ted leaned through the driver's window of the Toyota and said; "Now Simon, my boy, don't sit there all day, get down into the village and dig it up."

Instantly, Simon, with his Ford Mustang powered 360-degree excavator and Jaguar steering wheel, found himself in the stone circle of Avebury, or at least that was what it represented. Instead of ancient standing stones, there now stood tall pillars of cheese of every variety, Stilton cheese, Swiss cheese, Cheddar cheese and much more.

Using the excavator, Simon started digging, but each time he dug up some soil, the soil turned into some type of hard, crumbly cheese.

"Oh this is no good," he said, so he drove the excavator to a new spot and started to dig again, but this time when he tipped out the contents of the excavator's bucket, instead of cheese, thousands of red coloured butterflies flew from it. The air became so thick with them that Simon could no longer see what he was doing.

Next, the scene jumped to one where he was travelling along the open road from the village of Avebury in the red Jaguar. As usual, the normal physical dimensions of dreams still didn't apply, so this time, the red Jaguar had three front seats, instead of the usual two. Ted was driving the car while Miss Red Jaguar sat in the middle seat, wearing a pair of jeans and a red bikini top and leaning affectionately into Ted's arm.

Simon was sitting in the end seat. Miss Red Jaguar turned to Simon and said with some annoyance, "Well, Ted likes me," before turning towards Ted again and continuing, "Don't you, Ted, my love, my little telescope man you."

Ted clearly clearly appeared to be enjoying driving the red Jaguar and the female attention that came with it. He called across to Simon, "Sorry Simon, my boy, I should have told you about the red butterflies. I should have told you, but we ran out of time yesterday."

Miss Red Jaguar interrupted Ted, "Don't worry Ted, my love, he will have to find out for himself now. I bet he got your digger all dirty too." Then she turned and scowled at Simon.

"Right Simon, my boy, now let's see what this car can do."

And with that, Ted hit the gas and the second dream accelerated to its end.

An unknown amount of time went by before the third dream started. The third dream was a lot more vivid than the first two, and with somewhat of a more orderly, linear timescale of unfolding events. From the moment the dream started, Simon felt as if he was really living it, and it didn't quite feel like a dream at all.

He appeared to be in a time thousands of years ago when everything was more in line with nature and nature's laws. It was a time when less people inhabited the Earth and global industrialisation was still something totally unimaginable. The air smelled fresher, the sun looked brighter, and a natural positive energy could be felt flowing through all things.

He was standing there with a young woman beside him. They were both standing in front of a tall oak tree, which stood a short distance away from a great lake. The young woman beside him resembled the popular image of Pocahontas, with long, black, straight hair, that fell practically to her waist. Her face displayed a plain, but natural beauty combined with youth, while the rest of her appearance reflected a simple tribal life with limited possessions.

Carved into the side of the oak tree was a man's face, an image known in ancient times as the Green Man. This skilfully curved image of a man's face included hair and a full beard, all carved in the image of leaves from the same tree.

Simon and his Pocahontas turned to face one another while standing in front of this old oak tree with the rays of the morning sun reflecting light across the shimmering waters of the lake behind them.

"So this day we become one," he said to his companion. Then ceremoniously, he gently placed a headband made from small, white, wild flowers on top of her head. On receiving this, her face lit up with delight. Warm, loving smiles flowed freely between them. Simon's heart lurched in profound love and happiness as they shared this special moment in time. They both reached out their arms towards each other and held hands, in readiness for their vows.

"You are my woman. Where you go, I go."

"You are my man. Where you go, I go."

"I am your woman, now and forever, in this life and the next."

"I am your man, now and forever, in this life and the next."

Before speaking the final words, he produced a gold ring. The final words they spoke together. "As this great tree is our witness, we commit to live together as one as we play our part in the great circle of life." Then the gold ring was slid along her finger to its rightful place.

She held up her hand and they both looked at the polished gold ring as it shone in the sunlight. Then she looked at him, and he looked down at her, great joy twinkling in their eyes. She giggled and threw her arms around him. He held her as though she was the only thing he wanted in this life, pressed the small of her back, while she lifted her face to him, and he met her lips to seal their vows with a grateful, heady kiss.

She pressed her head to his chest, "Oh, my love, you are my man, at last, my one and only man. I am so truly happy this day to be joined with you. I knew from the first moment that we met that you would be mine."

"As did I know that you would be mine," he murmured contentedly.

The newly-joined couple walked together hand-in-hand, with the great lake and oak tree fading away in the distance behind them.

They stopped walking for a moment and she turned towards him, "Tonight, we can build a fire to keep us warm. I'll sing a song of love, just for you. Then we can lie together for the first time, under the stars, all night long, as man and woman. Oh, how I love you. You are my dream come true. We have only just begun our lifetime together and have our whole lives ahead of us. So much to do, so much to share together, so much of life to see and experience together as man and woman."

He looked deep into her beautiful doe-brown eyes, the windows to her loving soul. "I feel it too, my love, you make me feel complete. I would be nothing without you now. I am certain we were always meant to be together in this life. May the many summers and winters ahead of us bring us much happiness and good fortune. Tomorrow, we will arrive at my home, high up on the cliffs overlooking the sea. I am certain you will be happy there; it is so beautiful."

They both looked ahead and saw a tree on the horizon set upon a hill. "The weather has been perfect today for our ceremony and the first part of our journey to my home, but I feel a change is coming. Let's try to reach that tree by evening, and then we can build that fire you talked about and settle down for our first night together."

As they continued walking, she whispered softly, "I think there is a party of men some way behind us."

He also spoke softly, but reassuringly. "I believe you are correct, my love. I first heard them in the distance sometime after we left the lake. I did not say anything about it because I did not want to alarm you. They must be making good speed as they appear to be closer now than they were before. Don't worry, my love. I am sure they mean us no harm. Surely, they must only be travelling in a similar direction to us, that's all."

The dream moved forward in time. It was now much later that same day. The daylight was fading fast and the weather had deteriorated into greyness and mist. The couple walked up the hill towards the tree they had spotted earlier. They were both tired from their journey with the added worry of hearing the voices of the unruly men who appeared to be getting closer.

She asked as quietly as she could, "Do you think we have lost them?"

"Yes, I think we have lost our unwanted followers."

"They sound bad to me."

"I think you are right. I have not heard them for a while. Hopefully that is the end of it now, and you can lay your worries to rest."

Reaching the top of the hill, they stumbled on the uneven ground. Due to the mist, there was very limited vision of their new surroundings, making the tree very hard to find at first. Eventually, arriving at the foot of the tree, they threw themselves on the ground, exhausted and panting for breath. He rolled over onto his back and grabbed her towards him to rest in the crook of his arm.

Despite the long journey and the exhaustion, nothing could take from them the wonderment of this day as they both laughed in between gasps of breath.

But then, from somewhere out of the mist came a very wicked laugh, delivered slowly from a taunting, deep voice. They listened in horror as they realised that they were not alone. Slowly, they raised their heads to see in the mist the group of men in front of them whom they believed they had lost earlier that day.

Seven very rough-looking men were now standing directly in front of them. Dressed in a crude assortment of animal skins and leather, carrying knives and swords, they spoke a language not native to this land. Clearly, they had travelled far. They were all big, strong men, with a violent appearance about them.

In their own native tongue, they laughed and jeered at the young couple, now standing and holding tightly to one another in quaking fear of the unknown.

The leader of the pack walked over to the tree and ripped a branch from it with such uncanny precision that it came away looking like an almost perfect spear. The others laughed as if they had seen him do this trick many times before. The maliciousness in their laugh also foretold that they knew what would soon follow.

They returned their attention to the new couple, and the man with the spear used it to gesture for them to part. Instead, they both held on ever more tightly to each other, but they were easily overpowered by the seven big men and torn apart from one another.

In Simon's dream experience of being this young man, he put up a strong fight to protect his woman, but it was all in vain. He was no fighter in comparison to them, as the rough barbarians were very experienced in fighting, not just on the battlefield, but also for their own, sport, pleasure, and amusement. Very soon, this young man was conquered, beaten to the ground, and then kicked unconscious.

The scene moved to the morning after. Simon could see himself again in this dream. He was lying unconscious on the ground, as he'd been for many hours. Slowly, he came to and sat up, feeling very cold, with his body aching all over from kicks and blows he'd received.

Dazed and disoriented, he tried to recall the events that had led to this uncomfortable situation. At first, he could not recognise where he was due to the mist all around him, now thicker than it was the day before. Stretching out his arm, he could only see a little way past it.

Then, with great dread, the events of the evening before returned to him. He heard the sound of a man restless in his sleep. He started to tremble as he realised these men must still be very close by, somewhere in the heavy mist of this new morning.

Where is my young beauty? he thought to himself. He so much wanted to protect her and take her away to a place of safety. He scanned the scene with slitted, focused eyes, attempting to find her in the heavy mist. He could just make out the outline of the tree. Very slowly and as quietly as possible, so as not to wake the men sleeping nearby, he made his way towards the tree.

As the tree became clearer, he let out a gasp in great devastation. His eyes instantly filled with tears and he fell to his knees trembling. There she was, naked, a rope around her waist, binding her to the tree. She was motionless with the top half of her body leaning forward against the ropes. She had clearly been a source of cruel entertainment to these heartless barbaric men.

He stumbled to his feet. Again, he could hear the stirring sounds of the barbaric men waking, but he dared not look in the direction of these sounds. He needed to believe that she was still alive, that perhaps she was sleeping or unconscious, as he had been.

Creeping slowly forward, he made out the makeshift spear of the night before. It was bayoneted into her stomach. He fell onto his knees before her, the immense emotional pain shredding his heart, as he gasped for breath, trying to keep the moans from escaping him and alerting his love's murderers, as they would surely kill him too.

Tears fell unrestrained from his eyes, giving her an ethereal wavy appearance. Her left arm seemed to be reaching out towards him. She looked as grey as ash, but to him, she still looked as beautiful as ever.

Then came the scene that Simon had seen many times in his life. With tears in his eyes, he slid his hand over hers. It was ice-cold and lifeless. The greyness of the misty morning was everywhere, matching the hopeless misery of the day.

The voices behind him grew louder, informing him that these evil men were now awake again. He knew that he must leave immediately, or he too would soon be dead, but how could he bring himself to leave her? How could he live without her? More sounds could be heard behind him. He knew it was time to leave now, or else never.

With his hand in hers, he slid the wedding ring from her finger. With the ring removed, her lifeless hand fell without the support of his hand. Before fleeing into the mist, he kissed her cold, parted lips. He refused to say goodbye.

Next, played out the second image Simon knew all too well. He was standing in front of what appeared to be a large gravestone. The night sky was pitch black, apart from the flashes of lightning, as rain relentlessly poured down heavily from the heavens, matching the tears flowing from his eyes. The storm was dramatic with loud thunder and piercing lightning, combined with the sound of heavy rain hitting the ground.

When lightning flashed, the gravestone was illuminated momentarily, but no writing could be seen on this gravestone. Kneeling down in front of the gravestone, he dug away at the sopping earth with his bare hands, the hole filling with water as fast as he could dig it. With torn nails and raw and bleeding fingers, he dug to an almost arm's length in depth, and placed his love's gold ring inside the hole, before replacing the hole with the soaking wet earth.

He rose to his feet as the storm around him continued to do its worse, and with a wide range of powerful emotions raging inside of him, he shouted towards the sky, "I am your man, now and forever, in this life and the next."

Shaking with passion and rage, he continued shouting almost as loud as the thunder itself, "You are my woman, now and forever, in this life and the next."

Then, collapsing with grief, he fell to his knees on the muddy earth and quietly sobbed all his emotional torment as images of her flashed through his mind.

With one last blast of emotional energy, using all the remaining power within him, he defiantly shouted, "WE WILL BE TOGETHER AGAIN."

The power and energy released at that moment violently shook Simon awake, causing him to instantly bolt upright in his hotel bed, panting and covered in sweat. As his eyes began to focus, Simon saw Ted standing at the foot of the bed. He rubbed his eyes, somewhat aware of the tears in them, and leaned over to turn on the bedside table lamp before returning to look back in the direction of where he had just seen Ted. The low light of the table lamp revealed that there was no one else in the room.

The Universes Timetable

Chapter 9

For the next hour, Simon sat on the end of the bed talking into his new Dictaphone while drinking bottles of water to fend off the morning-after hangover. He knew the importance of not trusting his memory to recall the details of his dreams the next day, so he put everything he could remember into his Dictaphone while it was fresh in his mind.

When he had recorded everything he could remember from the three dreams, while also making note of having seen Ted standing at the end of the bed, he copied it to his laptop to keep it safely stored. "And that is why I see the scene of the ring and the hand and the second scene burying the ring. Now I understand," he commented aloud.

Simon felt a mixture of accomplishment, like he had touched upon some answers, and confusion, as those answers had only left him with more questions. He pondered for a moment about the final line from the dream which had woken him, "We will be together again." But how?

This young couple from ancient times may have been cheated out of their lifetime together, but, surely, there was no way to repair this wrong. Unless Grandad hadn't been losing the plot when he spoke of multiple lives, eternal soul mates, and out-of-body experiences. Simon had always believed that had Ted not been successful with his other business, he could have been a famous storyteller. As all the wild, amazing, and crazy things that had a tendency to spurt out of his Grandad's imagination at the same moment as his eyes would glass over and he'd seem to be somewhere else completely other than at his table in the garden, dishing out just another of his infamous talking moments.

That's why Simon had always, for the most part, been thoroughly entertained with Ted's talks, because they would always seem a combination of fact and fantasy, quite like folklore meant to teach very valuable information, all wrapped up in an entertaining fictitious story. Quite effective, really.

Such as when Simon had been 8 and Grandad had sat him down and said, "Simon, my boy, would you like to learn how to fly? Listen carefully, because the information I'm about to tell you is vital for you to successfully fly. There are steps to follow, each and every one of them important. First, you have to be as rested as one gets right before they reach the deepest parts of sleep. Have you ever heard the term, lucid dreaming, Simon?" Then Grandad had gone on quite a bit about that before telling Simon that that was the stage where he could leave his body and fly wherever he wanted. Simon, then, had clapped his hands in appreciation for having been told a fascinating tale.

"To just up and fly out of my body and all over the world, Grandad, wouldn't that be such great fun?"

"Not just all over the world, Simon, my boy, but to all the different times in the world, the past, the future." Then Ted's eyes had become lost in that other place and he'd said not another word.

"Well, I'll be," Simon grinned in the present. "That masquerading magician Grandad of mine had been trying to tell me all along. Is it possible that that was really me in the third dream, back thousands of years ago? It didn't seem a dream at all. It felt like I was there, experiencing it all in the flesh." At that, he touched his lips, still vividly remembering the contrast of her warm, plush, gentle lips when they'd kissed to seal their vows, and the cold, unpliable, lifeless lips he'd kissed before he fled his own guaranteed demise.

His heart still ached … profusely.

Never one for giving in to negative emotions or thoughts, Simon shook himself away from it. "Well, it is no good trying to get back to sleep again now - not with all these thoughts running around in my mind."

He put on his new watch and then looked at the time: 4:30am. "Well, time for a run, I think. I could go downstairs to the gym and use a running machine, but what shall I wear? My beach shorts and t-shirt are now the wrong image for me altogether."

Walking into the gym in his white cotton towelling Moonraker dressing gown and slippers. he did not look like much of a runner. The only other person in the gym was a young lady who was sweeping up with a small broom. "You are up early," she said in a Polish accent, pushing stray hairs away from her forehead.

"I couldn't sleep, so I thought a run would be a good idea." Simon kicked off his slippers to run bare foot on the running machine, then he noticed a book on a small table, so he picked it up before casually choosing a running machine. After a glance at the controls, he pushed a button and the belt of the running machine began to move slowly.

The cleaner observed him reading the cover of the book while running very slowly at the same time. Working at a hotel, she'd seen a lot, but watching a man attempt to run and read was one she hadn't encountered before, so she kept watching him. After reading the cover of the book, Simon tossed it towards the table he'd gotten it from. It landed nicely, but then slid onto the floor.

The cleaning lady scampered over to it and placed it back on the table, while wondering what this odd, yet fascinating man, would do next.

"Sorry about that," Simon said, not failing to notice the young lady's lingering eyes. *If multiple lives, reincarnation, were possible, was it multicultural?* Simon wondered. *Such that of a tribal woman coming back Polish? Or Miss Fiery Red Caucasian Jaguar to keep atop modern times.* After all, Simon thousands of years ago hadn't been sporting a fast ride or even a fancy horse, according to his dream.

"You don't look much like a runner, if you'll forgive me saying, sir," the young lady stated while sweeping the same spot.

"Oh I can run, believe me. I can run … I'm just warming up." Simon pressed another button and the belt went a little quicker. After a few minutes of this, he took off his dressing gown and threw it towards the small table, which first landed perfectly atop the book, but then slid off the other side of the table too. "Sorry, about that."

She instantly moved to pick it up and returned her attention to Simon, to see him running with only a small pair of tight black boxer shorts on.

"I believe I can force myself to watch this for a few more moments," she said with an interested smile on her face.

Thoroughly encouraged and entertained himself by his audience, Simon kept one hand on the controls and started slowly increasing the speed bit by bit as his muscular body rose to meet the challenge until he was at maximum speed.

He now looked like an experienced runner, his whole body animated and involved in the task. Simon noted that the young cleaner wasn't even bothering to pretend she was sweeping anymore, rather looking at him and smiling widely.

The momentum of Simon's progressive speed had him trying to run even faster than the machine would allow, now not stretching his limits, but the limits of the machine, and he went faster still.

The attractive lady took a step backwards as she heard the machine begin to make protesting mechanical noises. The machine simply could not keep up with this running man.

Simon knew the machine was no match for him, so he gradually eased the speed back down, until he was back at the slow pace he'd begun with while reading the cover of a book.

The cleaning lady couldn't resist a short burst of applause. "Wow, I have never seen anyone do that before. I hope you didn't mind my staring. You make it very difficult for a cleaner to focus on her task."

She picked up the dressing gown from the table and handed it to him once he'd stepped off the machine.

"The pleasure was all mine," he bowed with exaggerated English elegancy.

From the look on her face, clearly some speculative idea was forming in her mind, so Simon waited.

She drew in a deep breath and said quickly, "Would you like to come back to my room for a shower?" Her surprised and blushing face revealed that such an effort was out of character for her, the kind of thing she might think, but never speak aloud. She placed her hand to her lips and continued, "I cannot believe I just said that out loud, but now that I have, hell, why not?" She smiled bravely.

0-0-0-0

As tempting as the offer was, and how thoroughly Simon considered it, he wasn't one to take advantage of someone in the heat of the moment, especially since there was much more to Simon than tight black boxer shorts and the ability to outrun a running machine, so he took a shower in his own room and then dressed before heading back down for breakfast. Besides, he wasn't just looking to find someone; he wanted to find *the one* and though being petite like the Pocahontas in his dream, her fingers had been too large for the size of the ring he always visualized.

Entering the large dining room, he could see there was the option to take breakfast outside on the terrace, which overlooked the lawns and the River Avon. Although it was a nice morning, he chose to dine indoors. Looking at the menu, he considered eating something healthy, but opted for the Full English Breakfast instead.

He couldn't help but overhear a number of conversations from people around him. Many people were talking about yesterday's speech contest held in the hotel by the British Oratory Excellence Organisation, such as a group of women behind him.

"I thought Cerys Perenna really nailed it yesterday with her speech. I had her pegged as the winner. I was really surprised when she got second place," said a woman's gravelly voice.

"Didn't she give a speech for the contest last year, too?" responded a fast-talking woman.

Yet another woman, whose voice pitched high, said, "Oh yes, I remember, it was on the topic of the Law of Thinking. It was really quite amazing."

"She is a smart cookie that one; a very bright girl. Clever enough to make a big heap of money within a few years of leaving school; most people cannot do that over a whole lifetime," the first one commented.

"She is not someone to do something in the heat of the moment. She thinks things through to get the best long term result."

Simon smiled at this being said by the woman who rushed her words. Simon began listening intentionally as this Cerys sounded like a woman he might like to meet.

"Has anyone seen her this morning?" Inquired the third woman, and was followed with a quick, confident response.

"If I know Cerys, she will have been up bright and early this morning, running around the city streets of Bath, and I wouldn't blame her if she did. I bet it is lovely running around a city like this when you have the early morning streets to yourself."

Now Simon regretted using the running machine, and thought his time might have been a bit more productive running around the city. After all, you never know who you might meet, like Cerys, but imagine that – him running through the streets of Bath in just his boxer shorts. He would have gained too much attention, for sure, but not from the right sort.

An excitable voice that had apparently just entered the conversation said, "But hey, have you seen what she is driving now, or at least what she travelled here in? It would be very hard to find another vehicle just like that one, that's for sure."

Miss Red Jaguar suddenly popped into Simon's mind, reminding him of his dream of her leaning against Ted and talking to him reproachfully about waiting too long. Perhaps playing cat and mouse with her hadn't been a good idea. Timing was a funny thing. When was the right place at the right time really? Could it have been then in the lobby when she left her group to flirt with him? And like a fop, he'd said nothing. He could have at least asked her name. Surely, he'd see her red Jaguar again. Perhaps he'd take her up on that offer to race after all.

He moved on to a conversation that a mother and her teenage daughter were having as they walked by his table.

"Hey Mom, I heard on the local radio this morning that there is a new crop circle in a corn field somewhere near a place called Avebury."

Then Simon overheard an older couple sat at the table beside him as the older gentleman said, "That reminds me of the night old Tom died."

This made Simon perk up his ears when, instead of Tom, Simon had heard Ted, at first, until his wife responded, "Do you mean when Tom appeared in front of some of his family members the same night of his death?"

"Yes, there he was, supposedly dead in his own bed, but apparently his sister, who lived 50 miles away, had some kind of apparition of him, as if to say goodbye to her."

"Didn't Tom's youngest son get a visit from him that night, too?"

"So he claims, but I certainly do not believe in that sort of thing."

Simon's attention to the conversation was broken by a waiter clearing his now empty breakfast plate from the table while offering him a refill on his coffee.

Overhearing this final conversation led Simon's thoughts to Ted and that hundredth of a second this morning he thought Ted was standing at the foot of his bed. He wanted to believe his Grandad was just fine as he simply could not imagine it being any other way. A guy like Ted, surely the Universe had much bigger, ongoing plans for him. After all, Ted understood the importance of giving, and he knew there had to be balance in the Universe, and he'd certainly been given back to in kind from the Universe, but Ted just kept right on giving anyway.

Simon thought reassuringly to himself that what he saw probably had more to do with the cheese and wine, and perhaps the beer, too, but determined he should check on Ted anyway. He knew the first thing he'd say to him.

"Now, Ted, just because you have the ability to leave your body and fly to the moon doesn't mean that you should be helping yourself to my room without knocking, spying on my dreams again." Which then made Simon curious to know if Ted would know the new dreams Simon had had, so without further delay, he anticipatingly headed back to his room.

Simon was met with disappointment when he rang both of Ted's numbers and received no reply, so for the next hour, becoming increasingly more agitated, he alternated between calling Ted's mobile and landline numbers.

Simon's heart knocked against his chest as a growing realisation began to set in. Ted had been right about so many things, maybe, just maybe, he was also right about predicting his own death, too. Simon couldn't, wouldn't believe it, so he concluded he would return to Avebury. Perhaps then, Ted could finish the vital information he'd been meaning to tell Simon yesterday before being interrupted.

0-0-0-0

Walking out of the Moonraker Hotel through the main entrance and across the car park, Simon looked very well dressed in another pair of dark trousers set against a white silk shirt from Charringtons. Simon knew his Grandad would appreciate seeing more of his turning point unfold.

He checked the time on his watch: 10:30. It would take him just under an hour to get there. He scanned the car park. Of course Miss Red Jaguar's Jaguar would be there, saying she was still at the hotel, but Simon caught his eyes cheating the moment they fell upon the tiger-striped Toyota Land Cruiser, now parked directly beside his car, instead of one parking space away.

Alas, this time he couldn't linger in pure fascination at the unique vehicle and ponder over its owner, as he headed back out on the open road in his green Jaguar, the top down, on yet another bright, sunny day.

Upon arriving at Ted's, Simon pulled alongside Ted's Ford Mustang. He noted that the 360-degree tracked excavator hadn't arrived yet. Like the day before, Simon made the walk around the side of the house, but this time it seemed so much further away. Every step felt weighted, and no matter how quickly Simon tried to walk, time seemed to go in slow motion. His mouth was parched, and the silence of Ted's country-surroundings suddenly made Simon's thumping heart and short breaths very loud in his ears.

Finally, Simon made his way around the house where he could have a visual of the gardens. His instant reaction in spotting

Ted sitting at his table, his head overlooking an open book, was to fully breathe for the first time since arriving. He was just about to start jogging towards Ted when he noticed something else.

Ted was wearing the same clothes he'd been wearing yesterday – something Ted never did.

"Oh no," Simon whispered as he made the slow trek towards the bottom of the garden. As he got nearer, he saw that Ted wasn't bent over a book in his lap while reclining in his chair. He was slouching, cap over his face, as though sleeping, but almost exactly as Simon had seen him when he'd left the day before.

There was a red butterfly perched atop Ted's hand, which fluttered away when Simon reached towards the hand it was resting on. Ted's hand was cold. The same feeling as the lifeless woman's hand when the ring was being removed.

"Why, Ted?" Simon said sadly. "Why a red golf suit? I might have taken you more seriously had you claimed your departing day in your majestic-wear. Something, anything, other than that. A top hat, perhaps. That outfit you wore at our last holiday that made you look like a peacock."

Simon smiled in fond memories as all the images of all the varieties of Ted's outrageous outfits flashed through his mind. He took his seat beside Ted and reflected, in silence for an unknown amount of time, on all the happy memories he had of his Grandad over the years.

"Its journeys end for you now, my friend. If I'm to believe your words, perhaps we'll meet again in another lifetime. I can hope."

Suddenly the telescope moved to the original position it was in when Simon had first arrived yesterday. There hadn't been a breeze. Not a single one.

Ted's mobile phone started ringing, causing Simon to jump for its abrupt disturbance of the silence. He picked it up from the table and saw the caller name as Jayne Smith. Taking a deep inhale, he answered it somewhat solemnly, "Hello, Auntie Jayne. It's Simon here."

"Simon?" she said in surprise. "Is Ted all right?"

"I'm afraid not."

"Has he …" she paused. "Has he died?"

"Yes, Jayne - and he went peacefully, too, by the looks of it."

There was a long pause before Jayne spoke again. "I wondered if he had died last night, because I am sure he visited me in spirit, apparition, or something like that. Anyway, he stood at the foot of my bed dressed like a circus ringmaster, of all things."

Contained tears sprung in Simon's eyes. A circus ringmaster. Perfect. *That's the way to go, Ted, that's the way to go!* he thought, while she continued talking.

"Well, he certainly had a very unique dress sense; you could always say that about him."

Simon laughed, "Unique is what we're calling it, is it?"

After some time spent mutually reminiscing the life of unforgettable Ted, and his infamous talks, amongst so so many other things, the call ended.

Simon took responsibility in making Ted's final arrangements, though he was not totally certain who to call to report a dead person, so first he rang Ted's doctor. While waiting for the doctor, he rang a number of family members to inform them of what had happened, though most of them were themselves on holiday.

After a bit of time, the doctor arrived to pronounce Ted as deceased. Thereafter, the undertaker came to remove Ted's body from his beloved chair at his beloved table, holding his most prized collectibles, in his garden with its one living shrub. A shrub coloured with red from the butterfly atop it.

A number of hours passed unnoticed, as time seemed to stand still on such occasions as this. Simon hunted around to find the keys to the house so he could lock it up when he had finished. He then returned to the garden with a cardboard box and collected Ted's various things from the garden table. Simon saved the telescope for last, which he found was now pointing in the direction of Avebury.

Curiously, he looked into the eyepiece. At first, all he could see was an empty stretch of road leading towards the village of Avebury, but then a bright red Jaguar F-Type came into his view, and instantly Simon recognised the driver. "Ah, Miss Red Jag, how you do keep on showing up?"

He watched the car as it travelled into the village, until he lost sight of it. "Maybe she has gone to the village pub, or for a bit of sightseeing around the stones?" he pondered.

Now, with Ted gone, at exactly the time he had foretold, Simon felt more intent than ever to making Ted's final teaching words count. Perhaps he should drive to Avebury and see if he could track down Miss Red Jaguar.

After he had done all that he could at Ted's house for one day, he locked up and got back in his car. He revved the engine loudly and shouted above the noise, "This has been the only time I have left your house with a sorry heart. So long Ted."

He drove more sedately than yesterday as he travelled the lanes leading away from Ted's house. He shortly found himself arriving at the same T-junction with its two choices - turn left for Bath or right for Avebury.

"I think I will head to the Avebury village pub for a while and raise a glass to Ted. Maybe Miss Red Jaguar will be there and I will ask her to join me. Anyway, Ted wasn't someone who had time for sadness. It was always best foot forward with him, so now it is best foot forward for me."

The Avebury Ring

Chapter 10

As Simon made the drive towards Avebury, he felt that same sense of déjà vu he'd experienced at the airport – was it only yesterday? His mind could hardly grasp all the extraordinary changes made, and his total transformation, in only a mere week's timespan. All while he couldn't shake the feeling that this is how it had always been.

He'd always sported a green Jaguar. Always wore fine clothes. Always kept his hair trimmed and fashioned in a way that pulled off being casual, sexy, professional and refined.

Nearing Avebury, he felt the ease, relaxation, and security that he always felt, as if it was home and there was no other place he'd rather be. Simon shrugged off the feeling of déjà vu at being there simply because he'd driven through Avebury yesterday.

The feeling of home was probably memories of his years growing up, as driving through Avebury had always been part of destination Grandad, and the excitement Simon would always feel in seeing Ted again. For that, Avebury had always seemed a magical and joyous place, full of wonderment.

Simon had always found that this ancient monolithic monument, nearly a mile across, had a special soothing power and energy all of its own. It was divided by roads lined with houses into four individually-sized quadrants, circled by an outer ditch and bank earthwork known as a henge.

Although many people used terminology like quarter or section to describe each of the four main parts of the circle, Simon had always thought quadrant to be a more accurate term. Even though they weren't of equal size, they were all equally important and special.

Driving into Avebury from the south side of the village came with the luxury of seeing a good number of Avebury's ancient stones on either side of him as he approached the village pub in the centre of the village. After parking his car in the pub car park, he noticed the red Jaguar.

"Ah, Miss Red Jaguar, and here we meet again." Though coincidence, it was not, as Simon wondered if he would have chosen to drive to Avebury instead of back to The Moonraker in Bath if not for the telescope pointed in this direction.

He walked casually into the pub and up to the bar, pleased to see a very wide choice of beers, wines and spirits. He began to feel more and more uplifted and at ease while pondering his choice of beverage. Miss Red Jaguar wasn't amongst those sitting at the bar, so he turned to take a quick glance around the room. Sure enough, there she was, and could hardly be missed wearing a quite similar outfit to that of his dream, her wild curls splayed over her shoulders as she bent provocatively towards a big muscular guy seated at one of the pub's tables.

She seemed quite enthralled with her new catch. Any notion of romantic involvement with Miss Red Jaguar instantly vanished. Though she had been on his mind quite a bit since she had overtaken him on the open road yesterday, that particular bubble had abruptly burst.

"What can I get you?" an attractive-sounding female voice asked from behind the bar. Simon turned back to see a pretty-looking barmaid directly in front of him, but after seeing Miss Red Jaguar with someone else, he had lost his appetite for alcohol and was feeling somewhat deflated. He ordered a bottle of sparkling water instead, and took it to an outdoor table.

What next? he thought dejectedly while spanning the view around him. In looking at the stones, he recalled Ted teasing him about a favoured stone that Simon had had as a child.

"My thinking stone, of course," he perked up. "It's coming back to me now. Here's to you, Ted." He performed cheers by raising his drink in the air and drank his water down in one, then stood, knowing exactly where he was going next.

His thinking stone was in the northeast quadrant of the stone circle. Ahead of him was a middle-aged couple, dressed like people who were active country-walkers, while Simon, in his smart trousers and white shirt, looked somewhat overdressed for this place.

The man had a small open satchel supported by a shoulder strap with a pair of binoculars resting precariously on the side of the bag. Upon entering the gate, the couple turned left and walked along the fence towards the north. Simon carried on walking directly ahead, in a more or less easterly direction, which led him into the northern-inner circle of stones, known as The Cove, of which only a few stones still remained.

He admired the tall, grey sarsen stones as he passed them. Time had given them a very uneven surface due to thousands of years of weathering; small patches of fine moss clung to each stone wherever it could.

Simon continued past The Cove towards the far corner of the quadrant that featured a gigantic fallen stone that as a child he had personally nicknamed his thinking stone. Long ago it had fallen on its side, instead of flat on the ground, and the top of it leaned towards the sun.

Due to the northeast quadrant only having a few impressively-sized stones, it usually attracted less people, allowing it to be a quieter place than the other quadrants of the circle. As a child and young boy, he would sit on the stone and think things through in the peace and quiet this area of the circle offered.

He sat on it now, facing the inside of the northeast quadrant. He could see the couple now standing on the earthwork bank, admiring the sights around them. Simon moved to the long sloping side of the thinking stone and laid his back against it. He looked up at the sky and began peacefully watching the light, breezy clouds go by.

"Think. Think. Think, I had better think."

After a pause and some deep breaths, he began retracing step-by-step the events of the last few days. The dream that showed him his new green Jaguar that he'd purchased the following day, just as the dream had shown. Taking time off on a whim and planning a holiday. Walking through the airport with the déjà vu of having dreamed that Ted would call him, his planned holiday unravelling with Ted's "Hello Simon, my boy."

The only way Ted had convinced Simon to cancel his trip was his uncanny knowledge about Simon's dreams. Telling Simon he'd be dead the following day certainly helped make that decision to drive to Ted's instead of boarding the plane.

Sitting down with Ted in his garden, Ted very much alive, full of life, and seeming ages away from his death. For some reason, out of all the information Ted had been wanting to impart, he'd chosen to start with revealing his childhood ability of out-of-body experiences, which then moved to the Universe - the past, the present, the future – and the ideas of multiple lives or reincarnation, before reverting to disclosing more information about this *her* that Ted had inferred when they spoke on the phone at the airport. Simon's eternal soul mate. Perhaps Grandad had done it in just that way, knowing it would maintain Simon's attention for when he moved on to discussing Simon's turning point, the three stages, and the Laws of the Universe before returning to the subject of meeting *her* at exactly the right time and place.

Then, oddly, Ted seemed to begin procrastinating in revealing more to Simon, speaking of unrelated subjects, maintaining casual conversation as though he had all the time in the world, just as suddenly to end their time together the moment the telescope moved. "We are on the Universe's timetable now," Ted had said. And Ted had been right about everything up to this point, even his departure from this world.

What had led Simon yesterday to turn left towards Bath instead of turning right towards Avebury and heading home? And what had been the purpose of his turning right today, just to find Miss Red Jaguar no longer available? Simon reflected on his day and evening in Bath.

He successfully completed stage two in his turning point after letting go of the old Simon and creating the new Simon with a fine haircut and some nice clothes, and then experiencing himself as the new Simon. Staying at the classy Moonraker Hotel. Walking the streets of Bath and picking a place to sit outside and eat and drink as his newly-refined self to see what the Universe would attract to him. The beggar, the loud-talking Australian mate, the Japanese girls and the language-barrier over white horses and selfies, of which Simon had only succeeded in taking a picture of himself accidently.

His aimless walking to admire the sites while wearing off the buzz he'd drank himself into, all while being continuously harassed by the images of the hand and the burying of the ring until he became fed up enough to want to do something about it.

Spending the remainder of the evening engorging himself on delectable cheese and wine and falling into a deep slumber, two manifested dreams and then the one which had not felt like a dream at all, so vivid and powerful that it woke him straight up the moment he saw Ted's apparition at the foot of his bed.

His going to the exercise room at 4:30 in the morning and being tempted by the pretty, Polish, young cleaning lady's brazen offer. His time then spent enjoying breakfast and eavesdropping on other's conversations, which then led to his desire to check up on Ted, drive to his home, and say goodbye to his beloved Grandad for the last time. Now, here Simon was, lying atop his thinking stone, which he hadn't remembered in years, the prospect of Miss Red Jaguar a big disappointing fail, and no clue as to what he was supposed to do next.

"Ok, so where is my eternal soul mate then, Ted?" Simon said aloud in restless frustration.

Simon jumped back instantly to his feet when he heard Ted's familiar voice, "Simon, my boy, she is not very far away now, and as I said, it is vital that you both meet in the right place and at the right time, but what did you choose to *give*, Simon? The third and most important step. You must give to the Universe, so what did you decide to *give*, my boy?"

"My heart … and all the time in the world that it takes. I give my heart," Simon instantly replied, surprising himself, as just a second ago he hadn't a clue.

"I believe now, Ted. I believe!" He said excitedly, looking around for his Grandad who had to be there somewhere because he'd heard him loud and clear.

"Where the hell are you, Ted?" Simon stepped onto the stone to gain a little more height to see around him, but the only people in this quadrant were him and the middle-aged couple who had walked about halfway around the curve of the earth bank towards Simon.

"Now that's just creepy. I must be losing my mind. I think it must be time to move on a bit."

Simon ascended the side of the earthwork bank at its most easterly end and began walking on top of it towards the couple also walking on it.

White chalk dust from the ground began to cover his black leather shoes with a fine white dust. It was then brushed off when he walked through a section with long grass. He passed the other couple with a smile and a nod, noting the missing binoculars from the man's satchel, but not giving it further thought.

After passing them, he looked ahead of him along the remaining length of the bank, which he now had all to himself. Simon played Ted's words over in his head, though he didn't dare to speculate how he'd heard him to begin with.

"Well that is something anyway, saying she is not very far away now." His heart picked up its pitter-patter rhythm "So maybe I am very nearly at the right time and in the right place."

Finally, he came to the end of the earthwork bank, a section which finished on high ground overlooking Swindon road, with the northwest quadrant and the gates to Avebury Manor on the other side of the road. His mind wandered for a few moments, taking in the scenery. He looked at the stone gate posts of Avebury Manor, then he turned counter-clockwise just a little towards the stones on the northwest quadrant, the impressive Diamond stone standing nearest to him.

The Diamond stone had always caught Simon's imagination. He stared at the magnificent ancient stone for some time, almost as if waiting for it to speak to him, as many people have claimed these stones could do.

His gaze was interrupted by a red butterfly fluttering into view from his right. It looked very similar to the one resting on Ted's hand earlier that day.

"Oh, how the coincidences keep stacking up," he observed, "Well, one thing is for certain, if it hadn't been for Ted, I would not be standing right here, right now." The red butterfly continued its leisurely flight as Simon turned to follow it.

It fluttered its way to the ground, coming to rest on a broad dock leaf. Simon noticed something else almost hidden out of sight in the long grass. He walked towards it, and found it to be the pair of binoculars that belonged to the middle-aged man with the satchel bag.

He spun around to find the couple, only to see them walking back in his direction, clearly looking for the binoculars he now held in his hand. Simon held out his arm and waved the binoculars for the couple to see. They smiled and continued moving towards him. While waiting, Simon decided it a perfect opportunity to use the binoculars to look at the places too far away to see, as, from where he was standing, the village pub had to be a good half-mile away.

First, he focused the binoculars towards the wall of the pub car park, then he turned approximately 90 degrees to his right and landed on the gates of Avebury Manor. He turned back towards the circle, saw the raised earthwork bank of the northwest quadrant followed by the moat-like ditch in front of the bank before rising up again to ground level in the northwest quadrant. He kept slowly turning in a circle until the village pub car park was back into view.

"See anything interesting?" the middle-aged man asked from behind Simon. Simon turned back towards them.

"Thank you for finding our binoculars. Of course we did not even notice we had lost them until we were on the opposite end," the woman with gentle eyes said and reached for her partner's hand. Simon's eyes lingered on their entwined hands.

"It appears you may be looking for something yourself," the man said with amusement dancing in his eyes.

"Aren't we all," Simon smiled back. "What is that?"

An odd noise, different from the earlier sounds of the place moments before gained Simon's attention from behind him.

The noise grew louder as it drew closer, and Simon recognized it as the humming sound made by the wide tyres of a large vehicle, most likely a four-wheel drive, perhaps an old Land Rover or something similar. He looked in the direction it was coming from at just the right moment to see the tiger-striped Toyota Land Cruiser hurtling past him at probably 70 to 80 mph.

"Wow, someone is on a mission. Have the tiger's escaped?" he joked.

The Toyota held its speed well into the village before the brake lights came on, accompanied by the sound of the brakes screeching and complaining as they struggled to slow the old vehicle down before the right hand bend. The suspension of the old Land Cruiser was forced to its limits as the vehicle followed the road sharply round to the right, directly in front of the pub, instantly followed by an even tighter right turn into the pub car park just before coming to a sudden stop.

Simon could just barely make out the figure of someone dressed in black jumping out of the Land Cruiser and slamming the driver's door shut, the noise echoing throughout the circle. The distance was too great to make out much more detail, but luckily enough, Simon had a pair of binoculars in his hand.

"Have you ever seen such a sight, and what a ruckus. Someone apparently needs their alcohol," the woman commented.

Simon raised the binoculars to his eyes and sharpened the focus to reveal a very female form sprinting away in the opposite direction.

"She has a purpose, all right, but not the one you're thinking. Look at that, she just jumped the low brick wall of the pub car park and sprinted across the road without a thought to traffic. She's running like she's urgently trying to find something." Simon gave a play-by-play account to the couple whose binoculars he was currently confiscating. "But what on earth could she be looking for so urgently?"

Returning the binoculars to his eyes, he observed that she had stopped running and was standing on the outer side of the bend in the road, directly in front of a thatched cottage. This provided Simon with the opportunity to adjust the focus a bit more.

Now he could see that she was wearing a black business suit and that she had long, dark, straight hair almost down to her waist. Her hair was falling over her shoulders, so Simon was unable to see her face.

Well, we certainly have one thing in common. We're both the most overdressed people within the Avebury stone circle at this moment in time.

As he looked upon her, something began to happen. The solar plexus in the centre of his chest began to energise his whole body in readiness for something that it sensed was about to happen. His heart started to beat faster and his mind became more alert to each passing moment.

Then it hit him in the utmost shocking realisation that this was it. The right time. The right place. "Oh my God, surely it can't be her," he gasped. From that moment, time seemed suspended. He watched her frantically look in one direction over her right shoulder and then in the opposite direction over her left.

The slow motion of time was physically painful as second by second she slowly turned counter-clockwise towards his direction. Her arms, jacket, and long, dark hair all began to move outward, as she pivoted around towards the northeast quadrant of the Avebury Ring. Time now felt like it was going even slower still, a turn which would have been a brief moment in time for her, but for Simon, it took ages to unfold, and played out to the most miniscule of detail. Every split second feeling a minute as her face was revealed bit by bit, like looking through the roll of the film for a movie, frame by frame.

The moment her face came into full view, Simon was left without any doubt at all about who she was. His heart lurched and at the same time all his breath left his body. Tears came instantly to his eyes while he smiled larger than life itself.

'I give my heart … and all the time in the world it takes.' The words he'd blurted out suddenly a while ago came back to him.

"I give my heart," he hollered, unable to contain it within.

"What? What is it?" the woman asked.

At that unmistakable moment, real time came back instantly. Simon's heart was now violently pounding, "Oh my God! – I can't believe it. It's her. It's her. It is her! I can't believe it. Ted was right. Oh God, it's *her!*"

In total shocked amazement, Simon stumbled backwards, dropped the binoculars, and then tumbled down the embankment behind him. As he continued to roll down the bank, dirtying and wrinkling his fine clothes, being poked, prodded, and bumped by the objects on the ground, the only thing he could think about was the image of the girl he had just seen.

He came to a stop at the bottom of the earthwork bank. Quickly, he rose back to his feet. He felt his whole body tingle with excitement as adrenaline began to circulate his body. He had no idea how she could be here today in Avebury, but somehow, here she was.

He charged back up the earthwork bank and looked for her again. She was no longer standing where he had seen her only a few moments before. With a quick scan of the area, he spotted her running down the lane in an easterly direction, between the northeast quadrant, where he was standing, and the southeast quadrant.

Simon mapped it out in his head. *If I run across my quadrant towards the thinking stone, I can go through the gate in the corner and catch up with her. It is a good thing that I am a fast*

runner, and I already eased my body into it this morning on the
running machine.

At that, he began running, down into the earthwork ditch
in front of him, up the other side of it, and then he made a V-line
towards the thinking stone. He sprinted as fast as he could, all
while keeping his eyes on her. He so wanted to run faster, as he
knew only too well that he could, but here and there his leather
shoes would slip or struggle for grip on the grass. Even so, in no
time, he was halfway across the northeast quadrant, but then
suddenly, when she reached about three quarters of the way
down the lane, she jumped over the wire fence into the southeast
quadrant.

Simon immediately changed course and ran towards the
place where she had just jumped the fence. He jumped his own
fence in the northeast quadrant and landed in the centre of the
single track lane, causing a startled driver to honk his horn.
Without stopping, Simon hurtled over the next fence into the
southeast quadrant.

Due to a tall hedge, he lost sight of her momentarily until
he ran past it and found her already in the southern-inner circle.
She ran from stone to stone, touching them briefly, before moving
to the next one. Then she turned towards the southwest
quadrant, having not found what she was so urgently looking for
in this one.

By the time Simon reached the southern-inner circle of
the southeast quadrant, she had already entered the southwest
quadrant, and she was again running from stone to stone,
touching them, before moving on to the next.

Simon realised he wasn't getting anywhere by following
her when she quite obviously knew or had an idea of what she

was looking for, but just didn't know which quadrant it would be in, so he stopped running to see what she would do next.

After checking out most of the stones in the southwest quadrant, she turned and looked towards the gate leading to the northwest quadrant.

"If she goes into the northwest quadrant I'll be almost back where I started from," Simon murmured.

Sure enough, that was the direction she ran in next, so Simon opted for a shortcut that would place him in the northwest quadrant about the same time as her. He ran through the gate leading onto the high street directly opposite the village pub. He could clearly see her tiger-striped Toyota Land Cruiser in the pub car park, with a few people standing around admiring it.

He turned left and ran down the high street a short distance before turning right into a small car park. Reaching the top of the car park, he entered the northwest quadrant through the small gate. Something unusual that he'd never seen before was happening in this quadrant. About halfway between him and the Diamond stone, there was an archaeological dig in progress with a man and a woman working away inside of it.

A large pile of recently dug soil surrounded them and one of the sharp points of a pickaxe was embedded into the pile of soil.

Yesterday, Ted had mentioned that there was an archaeological dig in Avebury, and Simon was just remembering that bit of the conversation. Looking beyond the archaeological dig and the Diamond stone beyond that, he spotted the couple standing at the same spot where they had lost and he had found the binoculars. The lady was now holding the binoculars by her side and they were both watching with great interest and some bemusement, as if expecting to see some grand finale to conclude the chase they had just witnessed taking place around the stone circle.

A garden hedge was blocking Simon from being able to see the gate to the northwest quadrant. He heard the latch and hinges of the gate open and close, only a short distance away from him. He realised that she must be walking or at a standstill as she should have been a good way into the northwest quadrant by now.

Yes, there she was, now walking calmly and purposely by the stones along the outer perimeter of the circle, while focused on one of the stones ahead of her. She very much looked like someone who had found the place she had been searching for.

She remained oblivious of the fact that Simon had chased and followed her, unable to take his eyes off her. Now his eyes could confirm that she was most definitely the young lady he'd experienced in his visions, however many thousands of years ago, in front of the old oak tree. To him, she was, by far, the most beautiful girl in the world. This belief resonated throughout his whole body and was something now beyond question. Someway, somehow, their two souls that had lived all those thousands of years ago had been brought back into life through a dream and were now about to be reunited once more.

Though his heart was practically leaping out of his chest, as if trying to get to her, he remained still, slowly breathing in and out, feeling as though he had all the time in the world and he wanted to savour this moment, their meeting, their reuniting, until the very last second, just as he'd promised thousands of years before while raging upward to the skies that had themselves been raging too.

When she reached the seventh stone, about halfway along the outer circle, she stopped walking and turned back to look in the direction of the gate she had just passed through. She looked at each of the stones that she had just passed, before her gaze returned to the seventh stone. She had the look of someone trying to recall an experience.

Simon began to walk towards the seventh stone. Maybe seeing him would help her remember, but then her eyes continued roaming past the seventh stone, slowly, as if memorizing every single detail of every stone. They finally settled on the Diamond stone in the far corner of the quadrant.

The most wonderful smile lit her face, and with a nod of realisation and acknowledgement, her body became animated and she started to sprint towards the Diamond stone, her long hair flowing outward behind her.

Diamonds are a girl's best friend, Simon thought to himself while continuing to make his way towards the seventh stone in order to keep a clear view of her and what she intended to do once arriving at the destination she'd so urgently been seeking. He reached the seventh stone just before she reached the Diamond stone. Once there, she placed both her hands upon the stone and closed her eyes.

Time seemed suspended once more, so Simon did not know how long she stayed like that, but finally a gentle smile formed on her lips and she nodded her head once more, as though the stone had communicated something important to her in some way.

From there, the urgency returned to her as she dropped down on her knees in what appeared to be a very expensive suit and began frantically digging at the ground directly in front of the Diamond stone with her hands.

She yelled out some form of expletive that Simon couldn't quite catch as the ground was too hard to dig by hand. She knelt in thought for a second before moving towards the pocket of her jacket and retrieving an expensive-looking pen, which she then attempted to use to chip away at the ground, but no matter how much effort she put forth into stabbing the ground with the pen with one hand and clawing at it with the other hand, it was all in vain. The more she failed, the more frantic and determined she became.

"What on earth is she doing?" Simon said aloud while walking fast towards her before she hurt herself.

"My God!" he cried as the two recurring images flashed very briefly into his visual, but with a full screenshot instead of a widescreen. He'd thought it had been a blank gravestone. When the Australian had interrupted him, this was what the image had been trying to reveal to him about the surrounding area of the blank gravestone, because it wasn't a gravestone at all. It was one of the Avebury stones. And Ted hadn't been talking about Simon's fondness to the thinking stone. It was the Diamond stone!

The thinking stone that everyone knew about, is where he would go to think for brief periods of time, but the Diamond stone had fascinated his younger self in such an unusual way. How many times when he was younger had he knelt before the stone, just as she was now doing, remaining there for long periods of time, rain or shine, while Grandad had gone into the pub for 'just a moment, Simon, my boy. Be back in a jiffy'.

He remembered Granny touching his shoulder, saying in concern, "What is it, Simon? What draws you here to this stone every time we come here? It's a beautiful stone, for sure, but you do nothing but look at the ground. Tell Granny what you see, Simon?"

"It's not what I see, Granny. It's what I hear."

"Well then, what is it that you hear?"

"Leave the boy alone, my dear. Some things are best left kept to oneself," Ted had winked at Simon then and escorted Granny away, leaving Simon to his odd fascination with the ground in front of the looming Diamond stone.

"It's because I buried the ring there!" Simon cried aloud, and he could see it all now so clearly. The images no longer distorted and vague. He could feel the cuts on his fingers, little bits of rock and soil encrusted in his nails, the pelting rain, as though it was only yesterday that he'd found and then lost his one true love within 24 hours.

And there his true love knelt before the stone, very much alive, tears dripping upon the dirt she was so desperately trying to dig, trying to unbury the ring he'd buried so long ago. How she could possibly know was so amazing, it was beyond comprehension.

The right time. The right place.

"We will be together again," he'd vowed.

Simon began to shake and tremble with such powerful emotion.

He knew all the things that had transpired that led him here, at this time, to this place, but what life had she experienced up to this point? How did she come upon the memory? What had led her here, at this time, on this day and hour, to this place? Had he not woken so early in the morning. Had he not chosen to dine indoors instead of outdoors to overhear the couple talking that would lead him to think of Ted.

Had he taken longer before checking on Ted, or packed up the telescope first, instead of looking into it and seeing Miss Red Jaguar's car and deciding to drive to Avebury instead of returning to Bath to finish off his holiday. Had the couple not dropped the binoculars for his viewing pleasure, he probably would have mistook her as a madwoman or man. All these seemingly miniscule details had been designed for the both of them to be here right now.

The profoundness of it all was dizzying, so he refocused his attention on her, as each step took him one pace closer to her.

Since the pen, probably great for scrawling calligraphy, made for a useless digging tool, she desperately looked around her for something better to dig with before spotting the small pickaxe over by the archaeological dig. She ran as fast as she could, her mind appearing to want to run faster than her legs could carry her, to the centre of the quadrant. Like performing a relay race by herself, she aptly grabbed the pickaxe, pivoted, and sprinted back towards the Diamond stone.

The man working inside the archaeological dig site spotted her running away with his pickaxe. "You, Miss! You can't do that! This is an ancient archaeological site."

Just before reaching the stone, she dropped to her knees while still running, and slid on the grass before coming to a full stop in front of the Diamond stone. Although she was clearly unfamiliar with using hand tools to dig with, she almost-violently used the pickaxe to move the earth from in front of this stone.

After a few strikes to the ground, she freed up the soil enough to drag away a few large mounds of earth with the point of the pickaxe. From there, she used both the pickaxe and her hands to dig away at the more pliable soil beneath.

Suddenly, she stopped digging and cried out, a look of total astonishment on her face. Excitedly, she tossed the pickaxe high into the air over her shoulders, unaware that she had just thrown it in the direction of the archaeologist who was coming to retrieve it.

The archaeologist who had been running towards her stopped in his tracks, a wild look on his face as he tried to ascertain where the flying pickaxe would land. He stepped to his right, then, changing his mind, just as quickly stepped to the left, like he was dancing. It landed an inch in front of his foot. He cried out anyway in anticipated pain, even though it missed him, just barely. "You crazy woman!" he hollered, picking up the pickaxe to shake it in her direction, but wanting nothing more than to be away from her and whatever it was she was doing in his shaken state, so he returned to his colleague while venting loudly about having become an archaeologist because nothing that was dead in the past acted as insane as the living people in the world nowadays.

Unknown to him was that the woman he'd just deemed crazy had been the only one to unearth an ancient object from thousands of years past. She took hold of her pen and slowly lowered it into the hole she had just made. As Simon watched with growing fascination, she carefully lifted the pen. Dangling at its end was none other than a muddy, discoloured ring.

Simon felt his whole being stirred to its very core. He knew that this was the very ring he'd buried so long ago just as much as he believed that this woman on the ground close to him was the one he'd given it to.

Completely enthralled and amazed, she stood up, never once taking her eyes off the ring, looking very much like she was deep in thought with furrowed brows. She lifted the pen up to the light and looked at the dirty object on the end of it like it was the most glorious ring in the world.

Simon's thoughts raced through his mind. *If I removed that ring all those many centuries ago and buried it here in readiness for the day that we would be reunited again, and now here we are at this moment in time, though my dear beloved has yet to notice me, then I must be the one to place it back in its rightful place on her finger. But what do I say? 'Ah, there you go, you found it before I could unbury it myself. I believe this belongs to you, my woman.' I can hardly say that.*

Simon realised then that no words were needed as such words didn't exist for a time like this, so he moved his left hand into her field of view, underneath the hand she was holding the pen with. He heard her gasp softly. Without yet even looking at him, perhaps in as much shock as he'd been the moment he saw her, she tilted her delicate hand, now covered in dirt, and now sporting broken, jagged nails, which caused the ring to slide off the pen and into the palm of his hand.

Momentarily, they both gazed at this perfectly-shaped ring, its shape undistorted by time, though a dull green-gold with bits of earth encrusted to it. Simon knew this was the exact moment for their two souls to rejoin one another with a love that spanned the length of time.

Introductions were not necessary as they'd known each other literally forever throughout the Universe's eternity, just as they would continue to and always do so. Polite niceties and etiquette, a dinner and a dance, and kisses that grew in fervour after every successful date seemed ridiculous, though that was the way it had been up to this point and what every young gentleman was trained to do to win the girl of his fancy.

He placed the ring between his thumb and pointing finger and gently took hold of her left hand. She spread her fingers and seemed to jiggle her ring finger in anticipation of what he was about to do, all while she kept her head tilted forward, not once looking up at him.

He slowly slid the ring along her ring finger, holding his breath all the while. As the ring was slid past her fingernail, she inhaled sharply. Like Cinderella's glass slipper, it was the perfect fit for its rightful owner. They both released the breath they were holding.

A newly-formed tear from her eye landed directly on top of the old discoloured ring. They both looked up in amazement towards the ancient stone circle, as, like magic had just taken place, a small flash of light illuminated the area that alerted the tourists from all around.

Simon's attention returned to her when he heard her gasp. There before him, he watched the tear circle the ring, cleansing the dirt and discolouration throughout its course before reaching the place it had first landed and then falling towards the ground. This ring, thousands of years old, was now as bright and shiny as the day it was made.

She lifted her hand up again towards the sky, and the sun lit it up brighter still. But Simon wasn't looking at the ring. He was looking at her face, full of wonderment and joy. Unlike their past life when she'd been a tribal woman, all natural, having the limited supplies of only the necessities, he a survivalist and hunter, living remotely in the woods, as he could deem from the bow and arrows he'd been carrying on his back in the images revealed to him, he was looking at this life's incarnation of her for the first time.

She had the same features as before, but certain attractive lines on her face revealed that this life hadn't been easy on her. Much like her pricey business suit, she was very well professionally done up. Her dark eyebrows arched and trimmed immaculately, her deep black hair looking pampered like she saw a hairdresser at least once a week. The tears had not run her mascara on her long lashes and the ebony eyeshadow only served to illuminate the doe-brown of her eyes. The perfect heart shaped formation of her lips was only pronounced with the lip liner that matched the natural colour of her glossed lips.

She was absolutely spectacular and absolutely glowing in this profound moment. She began to slowly lower her hand, followed by her head, peaking at Simon between her fingers before lowering her hand completely and looking at him for this life's first time. Staring into one another's eyes, the windows to the soul, time became suspended once more, because both of them gazed at one another in the familiarity of having seen the others eyes a million times before.

"Ah, there you are," he murmured quietly.

Both of them were totally certain that they belonged to each other and always had. Their bodies moved towards one another, arms opening and reaching, all while looking nowhere else but at one another. Their fingertips touched first, and a feeling quite like a subtle static electric shock coursed through their bodies, accompanied by a sensation of weightlessness, as they both began to feel free of the restraints of earth for a brief moment in time.

His arms pressed around her back as her hands wrapped around his neck. He bowed his head forward and she tilted hers upward, and with but a gentle nudge at her back, their eyes closed and their lips met, joining them as one, one body, one mind, almost as if they were both two halves of one eternal soul.

A stream of unfolding images flashed through their visual minds of their many lives together throughout the eons of time and space, beginning with their most recent past lives.

He was a wealthy young gentleman in the 19th century and she was dressed plainly in a brown frock, and simple white bonnet, her long, black hair braided away from her face. He was standing on the bridge overlooking the River Avon, his horse and carriage parked alongside the bridge while she was down below watering her horse. In his hand, he held a locket, not of this century.

"What is the meaning of this? Why did you come to my home and give this locket to my servant?" he yelled to her from atop the bridge, holding out the locket.

"I was hoping you could tell me. I did not mean to intrude, but if you could just look inside it."

He opened the locket and found a picture that quite resembled him and quite resembled her, dated in the 18th century. Shocked, the locket slipped from his fingers and fell into the river. Without hesitation, she dove for it, in her simple but heavy gown. She would surely drown, so he careened over the bridge and went in after her. Pulling her to shore, both of them sopping wet, he yelled in a strong, refined English accent, "Are you mad that you would practically drown yourself over a trinket? Now that I have found you, my lady, I have every intention of making you my wife. Now I can't do that if you are dead."

While coughing the water out of her lungs, she smiled and said, "Pardon me saying so, sir, but I believe it was I that found you."

The scene jumped to his standing at the altar of a Bath Abbey, looking down the aisle, as she entered through the doors with her father at her side, wearing a very elegant white wedding dress lined with pearls to match the pearl and white lily headdress atop her head.

Then it was about a hundred years earlier. Simon was standing at another church altar in a small Wiltshire country church. He was dressed as a farmer, wearing a straw hat. Her father stood at the door of the church, tapping the side of his jacket to remind Simon of the loaded pistol he kept hidden on the inside pocket.

She stood before Simon, wearing a plain white summer dress, and a headband with hand-picked flowers. "My, I'm sure lucky to have found you. Prettiest girl I have ever seen. With that there locket, you belong to me now," he said, while placing the locket around her neck.

In another life, they were both dirt poor village yokels in the act of love-making in a field of corn, the summer sunshine sending its warm rays down on them both. Thereafter, it showed them walking hand-in-hand towards Stonehenge, the day of the summer Solstice when the sun rises as far northeast as it ever does, and sets in its farthest northwest position, beautifully silhouetted by the rich summer colours of the setting evening sun.

She was wearing a pretty, but simple, yellow summer dress, her hair pinned back with the red butterfly clasp he'd managed to barter for her in exchange for his shoes. He was wearing just some baggy trousers that were threadbare, sporting long stringy hair, quite resembling what Simon looked like just a few days prior to his turning point.

Next, Simon could see himself wearing an early soldier's uniform in a church that was a very small part of an army barracks. The father of the bride appeared to be of high-ranking, perhaps the General, as he handed his daughter proudly over to Simon. She was wearing a white Renaissance wedding dress, this time a dozen roses clasped into her hair around her head. With straightened frame and a huge grin, Simon saluted the father of the bride.

Further back in Roman times, an artist was rapidly painting the couple as they stood there as newlyweds. She was wearing a very attractive-looking Roman dress with one shoulder bared, all her long hair piled atop her head and held together by a multi-coloured gladioluses corsage, while he was dressed like a gladiator of that time period. The next scene jumped to them walking through the Temple courtyard of Aquae Sulis – the Roman name for Bath. Hand in hand, they entered the ancient thermal spring waters of Aquae Sulis and bathed in its warm waters.

Finally, it moved to the time Simon was familiar with, many thousands of years ago. At first, it showed him hunting. He could feel how very hungry he was. A sparrow cried out, alerting its whereabouts in the sky, so Simon readied an arrow and followed the sparrow with the tip, completely unaware of the girl running at him until she yelled, "Stop!" the very moment he was releasing the arrow, so it went wayward.

She was dressed in far less clothing, just enough to cover her feminine secrets. Then they were standing by the old oak tree near the lake, making their vows together. "As this great tree is our witness, we commit to live together as one, as we play our part in the great circle of life." The gold ring was placed upon her finger.

Simon felt a bit of vertigo when it revealed them flying through the air as birds, so close that their small, feathered wings almost touched. They glided freely through the air, soaring and swooping while communicating secretly through a type of mind connection. They spotted a tree. He landed on the branch closest to the tree as she landed towards the end of the same branch. Then they played this game of his hopping closer to her, looking straight ahead, her hopping closer to him, looking straight ahead until they were tucked up tight next to one another. Then she began singing a love song.

Simon could now feel himself living as the tree, but there was another tall, mature tree standing by his, many of their long branches intertwined and supported one another. He could feel the breeze blowing through the branches, the sun roasting the leaves that a little bit of rain would cure, the unique experience of breathing through the leaves, the amazing sensation of feeling his roots, deep in the ground, drawing life energy directly from mother earth herself.

He could feel himself reaching for the other tree and could feel her reaching for him, as the more years they had together, the more their branches wrapped around one another. He watched the pesky caterpillar that had been taking bites out of his leaves finally become the red butterfly that would tickle his leaves instead. Both trees felt the breeze change in direction, and could sense open water nearby.

Instantly, they found themselves floating on a lake and living as two white swans, paired for life.

A vast assortment of images continued to flash through their minds, revealing countless past lives, here on Earth, other worlds, other dimensions, living as people from all walks of life or beings in other worlds, living as animals on land or under the sea, as a number of plants, but always together, true soul mates through the eternity of time and space. A love like no other. An eternal love. One that would never fail them.

The images then began to reverse, faster and faster, now moving from past to present.

His branches of the tree now almost completely enfolding her, their beautiful leaves fallen, he felt the first pain of the axe cutting into his thick trunk. Over and over and over again. He felt himself dying. The branches of her tree held him up as long as she could, but her branches began to fall from the weight of him. His trunk, now unable to support itself, leaned against her trunk, but he was just too heavy. He plummeted to the ground.

In the next life, they were soaring again as birds, but this time with a sense of danger, darting in and out and flying as fast as they could. An arrow pierced through her breast and she toppled lifelessly to the ground.

Simon watched with pride as the next image revealed her departing words before being speared to the tree. She was relentless in her fight, clawing at their arms and faces as they tried to have their way at her, and when she no longer had her arms or feet to use, she used her teeth, making their attempts quite painful in the process. She'd even stabbed two of them with a small stone dagger she'd kept strapped inside a pouch wrapped to her waist. "I belong to my man and my man alone. You will have to kill me to take this body."

Then just as the spear penetrated her stomach, she reached out her ring hand and said, "I will find you again, my love, in the next life."

The Roman life, revealed them aged, Simon's body racked with pain from his many battles as a Gladiator. Their painted portrait hung crooked on the wall. She pleaded with him to retire the life before going into his last battle, which was his downfall.

Then he was back in the army barracks, all of them awoken abruptly by the sounds of screams, and the thick smoke of their lodgings being burned. When all the other guys were filtering out as fast as they could to get to a place of safety, Simon was extracting something from a hidden place he kept. It was the portrait of him and her from Roman times. So focused on this task, he didn't see the enemy sneaking towards him until he was bayoneted from the back.

As the dirt poor village yokels sneaking time together in the cornfield, her father caught them together and shot him on the spot. He died in her arms. She buried him in that cornfield at their special place with a small stone marking and planted buttercups to grow around his grave, the only buttercups in a field of corn.

The farm he had purchased as a farmer revealed acres of hay, but for one spot that grew buttercups. It revealed her dying giving childbirth, him holding her hand, alternating between telling her to stay with him and yelling, "Where's that God dang doctor?" while their five other children stood outside the room. As she took her dying breaths, she said, "Don't bury the locket with me. Keep it somewhere safe. Promise me."

Then the final scene of their last life as being a wealthy couple in Bath, standing outside their mansion engulfed in flames, when suddenly, she dropped his hand and started running towards the house, saying, "The pearl-and-lily headdress." Him chasing after her, grabbing her arm, trying to yank her back, and her stubborn insistence.

"How will I find you in the next life?" she hollered while breaking free from his grasp and running into the burning house seconds before the second floor collapsed.

Finally, Simon and she broke apart from one another, gasping and looking towards the ring as though to conclude everything they'd just seen and experienced with their first reuniting kiss.

"Oh wow! You are … You are my soul mate all right," she said breathlessly, eyes wide.

"As you are mine," he returned giddily. Then he embraced her more tightly. "I've lost you so many times."

"We always found a way to find one another again," she said dazedly, glancing once more at the ring before returning her eyes to his. "It appears we just can't seem to get enough of one another," she teased.

He abruptly moved apart from her and extended his hand, "Simon. Simon Tesla Templeton. That is my name in this life."

She giggled at these backwards turn of events. "And I am Cerys Perenna. My last name means -"

"Eternal," Simon finished, surprising her. "My Grandad taught me that. Anna Perenna, the Roman Goddess of long life, and renewal, health and plenty. The cycles of life -"

"Endings bring new beginnings," Cerys finished, so much love held vivid in her eyes while Simon wanted nothing more than to have her back in his arms.

"Heaven is the moment I look into your eyes," she murmured."

"Forever just simply isn't long enough to hold you in my arms, but I suppose I'll just have to be satisfied with that. Shall we be married then?"

"Let's try another kiss, and see if we can soar again."

Simon smiled lovingly at her, "Let's do just that."

From the Author

When I go on holiday, I like to take a few books with me. I usually first choose a book for the airport and flight out to my destination, followed by a few other titles to read while relaxing in the sun. I soon noticed after my first few trips aboard that holiday-makers like to share books after reading them.

One hotel we stayed in some years ago in Tunisia had a small table at the end of a corridor leading to some of the guests' rooms. Each day someone would place a book they had finished reading on this table. A while later, the table would be empty again, then at another time a different book would turn up. Some hotels even have lending-libraries full of well-read, used books.

I have also witnessed, on a number of occasions, people personally offering their finished book to another stranger to read. I like this concept of sharing books on holiday, and will leave my finished books for others to read, recycling at its best, to avoid it just sitting on a shelf while I endeavour new reads.

Over the years, this experience of book sharing on holiday has been part of those thoughts and memories which regularly drift in and out of my mind. Then one day in mid-March 2016, just a couple of weeks before my 50th birthday, I started to give the idea of writing a book designed-for-sharing some serious thought, and from that point on, in no time at all, the idea began to come alive. The book title and cover design soon came to me, the content and chapters became clear to me. New and original ideas to promote and distribute this book came into my mind and within a few days of exploring the idea in more detail, the book almost began to write itself. I found myself writing down detailed notes, which were very soon being written into chapter content. I became very excited as it increasingly dawned on me that The Well-Travelled Book

Series was going to be a ground-breaking book, a real first, in so many ways, and people could have some real fun with it too.

Where has The *Well-Travelled Book* travelled to, been read by, and when was it read?

In the following pages, there is a section where *The Well-Travelled Book* tells of its travels and adventures. Each reader of this copy, can, after reading it, take a pen and write in the book, their name, where they read it, and when they read it. As the list of readers, dates, and locations grow, this section of the book will become a fascinating read, as this book will then tell the reader all about its well-travelled life.

Just to add to the fun, why not post a photo / selfie on social media of you reading this book, wherever you are reading it. Or you can find *The Well-Travelled Book* Series on its own Facebook page and post a photo and some details as to where your copy has travelled so far.

After reading this book, please sign and date it, and then share this book with another person.

The Well-Travelled Book Series

To read other titles from The Well-Travelled Book Series in paperback and on Kindle, or to post a book review, please go to –

www.amazon.com

or

www.amazon.co.uk

There is also a Facebook page for *The Well-Travelled Book Series*

Where Has This Book Travelled?

Please fill in your name below and then share this book with someone else.

Maybe take a photograph of this book in whatever part of the world you have read it in, and then post it on social media

Names of people who have read this book	Date	Where this book has been read and travelled to

39979921R00099

Printed in Poland
by Amazon Fulfillment
Poland Sp. z o.o., Wrocław